The Sword of Allah

The Sword of Allah

Kent Kloepping

Dusty Lane Memories   Tucson, Arizona

This edition was prepared for publication by
Ghost River Images
5350 East Fourth Street
Tucson, Arizona 85711
www.ghostriverimages.com

ISBN 979-8-218-24695-2

Library of Congress Control Number: 2023913538

Printed in the United States of America
August, 2023

Contents

This book is dedicated to

MARLYS
When one we cherish passes, it is only then we certainly
understand all they gave to us in life and what we have lost.

*Only remember this: To seek justice
is a good and noble thing. To
seek revenge, out of hatred, is
something that will devour your
very soul.*

James Mace

GENESIS OF HATE

Ishmael Abboud: 1961-1965

For as long as he could remember, Ishmael knew the Jews, the Israelis, were terroists, butchers and the enemy. It was true because his father had told him; besides his father was a devout, faithful follower of Islam and the one true God, Allah. Sometimes he would ask his father why the Jews did terrible deeds, especially directed toward the followers of Muhammad. Why are they "subhuman" as his father often repeated.

His father would carefully explain how the Jews had come into their Islamic home and taken the land, killing many innocents with their treachery. They did not worship Allah, rather a strange being they called Yahweh. Ishmael knew when he had asked too many questions as his father would pause, stare intently at him with his black eyes blazing and say "my son this is so and the truth comes from Allah; do not ever question the righteousness of his wisdom."

While his father was the unchallenged master of their home, mostly always stern and sometimes even harsh, his mother by contrast was soft-spoken, fair skinned with sparkling blue eyes. He knew her name was Susan, but he always called her mother. When he asked her if Allah was also her God, she would reply "your father is the one who knows the true path to eternity and as his wife, and son, we must follow where he leads us."

He did not understand what she meant, only that it was a question not to be repeated.

Susan Hendrickson, Danish, was a University of California Berkeley liberal thinker, the daughter of a wealthy legislative bureaucrat and his wife a schoolteacher. Susan had gone to Cairo, Egypt on spring break with several other sorority sisters, also from wealthy families. Roaming, sometimes recklessly throughout the city, one evening at an upscale restaurant she began flirting with a strikingly handsome man she noticed was watching her. 'Oh my goodness' she thought to herself, 'that fellow is forbidden fruit.' The man was Gamel Abboud, soon to become Ishmael's father. Although he drank no alcohol, Susan did and eventually his charismatic charm lured her into a sexual relationship which ended in her pregnancy. She didn't return to Berkeley and eventually married Gamel in an Islamic ceremony.

Ishmael loved her deeply; she was always there to comfort him whether he was ill or retreating from the sternness of his father.

Ishmael's father was a decorated Colonel in the Egyptian Air Force, a superb pilot, well respected among his colleagues and a favorite of the military establishment. He was tall swarthy, with dark skin, a muscular frame and piercing coal black eyes. He excelled athletically and was fiercely competitive in all endeavors in which he participated. He had high standards and expectations, not only for himself, but additionally for his wife and only son, who he often referred to as his "golden child from Allah." Thus Ishmael's interests, activities, even his leisure time and playmates or friends were carefully screened and approved by his father.

One evening when he was six years old in 1961 his father ushered him into his study saying that he needed to have a "talk" with my son. When his father summoned him in this manner he knew the topic was important and might not be positive. Indeed both the topic and his father's discussion were a shock to Ishmael.

"Ishmael you're going to have the privilege of attending an outstanding school to further your understanding and knowledge of Islam."

"Where is the school father," he asked?

"Well, it is in South East Asia, a country named Malaysia; it's a private Tahfiz school(Tahfiz meaning memorizing, the Quran), where I'm sure you'll learn the true meaning of Islam."

Ishmael was devastated and his father seeing the dismay in his face asked, "are you not pleased with this wonderful opportunity?" Ishmael knew he could not reveal his true feelings of despair. Instead he weakly stammered,"oh no father it's that it's just such a surprise."

"Good, then you need to speak with your mother about all of the things you will need on your journey."

When he found his mother he began to sob; "oh mother I don't want to leave you and go so far away."

"Now, now dear son you won't be gone that long, maybe a year or two; it's a wonderful gift your father is giving you."

"But can't you tell him I'd rather stay here with both of you?"

"Ishmael you must know that your father has only your best interests and future in mind with his decision."

"Mother, you could talk to him and explain that I'm so happy here and will promise to learn all there is about the prophet and his teachings."

"I understand what you must be feeling, but your father has made the decision and I cannot and will not challenge him on the matter."

When Ishmael stopped sobbing and thought of what his mother had said, he suddenly thought of her in a different way. She didn't support him, rather simply followed what his father had decided. He felt a sense of loss and abandonment. He thought, 'is my mother weak, not strong like my father? Are all women that way'?

Ishmael would later recall that the four years he spent in Malaysia he was terribly lonely and mostly felt alone and betrayed. However, he compensated by ferociously immersing himself in the study of the Quran. His instructors were astonished at his remarkable ability in memorization and retention for such a young child. When he returned home at the age of ten his parents were also amazed at his comprehension and understanding of his Islamic faith. He also presented them with a commendation from the school that identified Ishmael as the most outstanding student to have ever attended their institution.

Once at home, Gamel immediately not only hired a cadre of academic tutors but also initiated activities for Ishmael that he termed would lead his son on the road to "manhood."

He enrolled Ishmael in local competitive athletic events and games as well as supervised recreational activities. Under his father's watchful eye and carefully selected trainers, Ishmael rapidly developed into a skilled athlete, particularly in futbol, cricket, and swimming. He regularly participated in athletic events with established secondary schools, even though he did not attend the institutions. Given his highly developed athletic skills at such a young age he was always welcomed as a member of the team. However, it soon became evident to him that his teammates viewed him as an "outsider." He was never a member of the fraternity or the "gang." Although he enjoyed the competition, particularly winning, he harbored a continuing pervasive sense of not belonging.

Notwithstanding, his father continued to pressure him to participate in team oriented athletic activities. Also daily study of the Quran was required with recitation of extensive passages from memory.

" So you will never forget the words of the prophet," intoned his father. Gamel also felt it was time for Ishmael to learn the history of treachery by the Jews against the followers of Islam. He developed a study guide (his version) of atrocities by Jews during the years 1931 to 1948 in the Palestine Mandate and then in Israel.

His focus was on the operations of Irgun, the radical offshoot of the Jewish paramilitary organization Haganah. Irgun was responsible for multiple attacks aimed at not only the Arabs but also the British. One of their favorite tactics was bombings. Two well- known egregious terrorist acts were the bombing of the King David hotel in July of 1946 killing ninety-one individuals of various nationalities; however, the second, a focus of Gamel's vitriolic spewing was a detailed and in-depth study of the Deir Yassin massacre on April 9 1948. Despite having earlier agreed to a peace pact, over 250 innocent Muslim men, women and children were slaughtered. Later estimates reduced to the death toll to one hundred+, but Gamel insisted the higher number was more accurate. His teachings included graphic details of rape, brutal beatings and summary executions. After each lecture Gamel would admonish Ishmael, "you must never forget the atrocities and heinous acts committed by the Jews at Deir Yassin."

Gamel had indeed provided strong foundational building blocks for Ishmael's future academic/athletic achievements, as well as his adherence to the tenets of Islam; equally important to Gamel was his feeling that he had successfully planted the seeds of hatred for all of Judaism deep within the soul of his ten year old son.

GIFT FROM YAHWEH

Foehrenwald: 1947

David Landau was born at Foehrenwald displaced persons camp in the late summer of 1947. His mother Naomi was the lone survivor of the Landau family from Cologne Germany. She and her husband Benjamin, a highly successful gemologist and their three children, lived a comfortable life in that wondrous city of Westphalia. But in July of 1942 a national madness, that had become endemic throughout all of Germany, arrived at their home in Cologne.

It was early morning and there was no sun. The sky was a dull aluminum gray and a light drizzle was chilling everything; it seemed that the heavens were weeping not only for the landau's, but for all of Judaism. The Nazis came, took their home, all of their belongings and relocated them to "so called Jewish house's," as they awaited further deportation to a concentration camp. After three long years of unspeakable terror (1942-1945) during which her husband Benjamin and children Peter, Lydia, and Ernst perished, Naomi was liberated from Auschwitz and arrived at Foehrenwald In June of 1945.

The camp was one of the three largest displaced persons camps in Germany and the housing conditions there were far superior to the others. There were 3000 people in the camp in the summer of 1945 and many of them seemed almost carefree and happy. They were free to move around the camp and enjoyed the ability to practice their religion. The camp had a rich educational and cultural life; schools for children, a vocational training institute and a Yeshiva, (religious academy) for young people. There was a great deal of interaction among residents in the camp; testimoy to that fact was the many marriages and new babies born within fifteen months after opening.

However, living there for Naomi, more accurately surviving day to day, continued to be dreary and depressing. She often contemplated suicide as she struggled to find meaning for existence and why she was alive and all of her family gone. Many others adapted readily to the conditions in the camp, but not Naomi. As she and the other residents were not allowed to leave the camp, the confinement sometimes brought back terrible night time dreams of the horrors of Auschwitz. Sometimes she awoke screaming and at other times sobbing hysterically.

There were many in the camp who approached her with encouragement to become involved in differing activities of the camp. She was treated well by all, but could not break out of the seemingly iron cocoon that enveloped and protected her. For over ten months she maintained her emotional and psychological distance from others and did not participate in any organized activities. However, in recent months she began to experience days without depression.

Then one sunny spring morning in 1946 Naomi was feeling almost cheerful when a man who appeared to be about her age, said to her "goede morgen, mooie vrouw" (good morning beautiful woman) in her original Dutch language. She was startled, not only by the language but also what seemed to be his brashness; she didn't respond which elicited a wide smile and a question, "is everything okay my lady?"

"Oh no, I'm sorry, I just wasn't expecting a greeting in Dutch."

The slim, but well built man had a long mane of blond hair and sparkling blue eyes. His engaging smile and a pleasant demeanor immediately softened her often defensive protective posture.

"Well please forgive me, I have seen you before and meant to say hello. My name is Kennet Kloster and I am from Holland, although I was born in Denmark. What is your name, if I may ask?"

"Why my name is Naomi, Naomi Landau."

"Naomi, that's a beautiful name, which I love, as it was also my mother's name."

Naomi tensed a little, wondering if he was being truthful or trying to gain favor with her; she didn't respond and Kennet changed the subject. They continued to chat for awhile and she learned that he was also Jewish. Before parting he asked her to have coffee with him one morning and to her surprise she agreed.

A week later they met for coffee and during their visit Naomi remarked that the name Kennet (Kenneth or Ken in English) was an unusual name for a Jew.

"Aha, laughed Kennet, you see my father had some Scottish blood, loved history, and had an ancient hero, King Cinaed (Kennet) McAlpin, who united the Scots and the Picts in the ninth century; so he named me Cinaed or Kennet in Danish."

Ken, as Naomi now called him, continued on with more history of the great King of Scotland who's regal name he carried.

They began to meet on a regular basis, and every time

they parted Naomi felt a sense of calm and of being uplifted. Without recognizing what her feelings were for him, she began to look forward to seeing him; soon on a daily basis. During the following months their relationship continued to grow, but Naomi continued to maintain her emotional distance from him.

One day after a particularly enjoyable encounter when she had laughed delightedly at his antics and storytelling, a new and long lost sensation filled her heart; it occurred to her that she was in love with this free-spirited fellow. He was kind, full of life, still able to find joy in each day, optimistic for the future, and besides all that a handsome, devilish companion. His ability to look beyond their current circumstances and see a future had been a balm which had begun to heal some of the terrible psychological abuse and emotional wounds that began in Cologne, the Lodz ghetto, and ultimaely in the unspeakable brutality of Auschwitz.

He was full of stories of his youth and many mischievous antics. One of her favorite tales was of him learning to literally run up a tree trunk, grab a lower branch and pull himself into the tree. She questioned him about the truthfulness, and to her amazement and the hilarity of many others in the camp he proceeded to demonstrate the technique.

He told her that he was a great hunter; there wasn't a duck, goose, rabbit or any other edible critter that was safe if they came within fifty yards of him. He said he was extremely ac-curate with a shotgun and used to win shooting contests. The only time he lost was when an older brother, who could likely outshoot anyone in Holland, was in the contest. Naomi loved every story he told her, but would usually ask, "oh Ken is all of that really true?"

"Of course it is, and besides all that I was a great skater; when everything froze in the winter I could out-skate all my classmates in school and eventually the entire community. I was faster then anyone; but that's not all, I could run like the wind and had unending stamina. His storytelling didn't sound arrogant rather just straightforward and matter of fact. She did love the stories, but would often tease him that he was sounding a bit boastful, then she would laugh.

They became inseparable and in early 1947 Naomi became pregnant and her son was born later that year. She was initially upset and frequently cried, but Kennet sat and gently comforted her; he said "Naomi don't be sad, maybe this child is a gift from God so that you can have a new family. You have lost much but Yahweh will never abandon you. It is his sign to you that you have a future and will again find happiness. You must be strong for him for our future together is uncertain."

His words were prophetic for in the Autumn of 1947 he was repatriated to Holland. Naomi grieved for a time for this man who had helped her heal the past devastation in her life.

Her son, David, was a strong healthy child; he walked at only 10 months old, and begin speaking after only one year. But tragedy once again struck; David along with others in the camp contracted poliomyelitis. He was very ill but to the amazement of the doctors in the camp he recovered rapidly, although with permanent paralysis in his legs. He adapted readily to his limitations and was extremely creative in finding ways to continue participating fully in the daily life of the camp. It was apparent that he was a unique child, intellectually superior to his peers, but at the same time a happy, gregarious, fun-loving boy. Early on he demonstrated an almost intuitive ability to recognize and understand the feelings and thoughts of others. Naomi realized that Yahweh had indeed given her a very special gift. She also eventually found closure in losing Ken and realized that in fact he had saved her life. When she thought about all he had been to her and what he had said to her at the birth of David, she knew he was right.

Alone one night, she lifted her hands heavenward and spoke the following to acknowledge her Creator.

"Yes, I will raise this child and take him to our new home. I shall call him David Kloster Landau."

In 1950 when David was three years old, Naomi and her son went to Israel.

PRANKSTER TO PRIVATE 1st CLASS
Will Panzer: 1948

Will Panzer was born in 1948, the third son in a family of four boys. His parents were hard working German Lutherans. Early on it became apparent that little Will wasn't the compliant son as were his siblings. Within the first two years of his life his personality began to unfold. He was a mischievous child, then a youthful prankster and eventually as an adult, the author of escapades that were classic. However, as a small child neither he or any of his brothers rarely ever challenged Heinrich Gustav Panzer, their stern father. Will, even at an early age considered the idea, but fearing the wrath of his father he most often thought 'maybe at a later time.' Will adored his mother Catherine, a slightly built dark-haired beauty. She would always forgive him, gently saying," I love you Will, but you must try to be a good boy."

He began elementary school at Saint Marks Catholic School. In his first two years he did spend time in the principal's office for noncompliance with various school rules.

Tragedy struck the family when Will was only eight years

old; his mother was killed by their huge Holstein bull and Will witnessed the mauling. His rat terrier dog, Rascal, had charged the bull and instead of attacking the dog the enraged animal chose his mother. Will was helpless to intervene as he watched the ferocity of the animal crushing the life out of his mother. He never totally got over her death and his feelings that somehow he was partially responsible for the incident. A year later his father married a local spinster from their church congregation, Freda Schultz. She was a strict God-fearing woman and she and Will instantly disliked one another. Freda took her role as stepmother seriously and preceded to work at "straightening out" young Will. Her efforts only made the relationship worse and Will more unwilling to follow the rules.

Throughout Will's elementary school days he was often singled out as the perpetrator of pranks in school; sometimes correctly, on other occasions he was innocent. Then one evening at the dinner table, during a casual family conversation, his father mentioned the establishment of a new facility for juvenile delinquents in the twin cities; also known as a reform school. Coincidentally there seemed to be a dramatic decrease in the incidents of Will's shenanigans, particularly at the school.

However, when Will entered high school he again began to either instigate or participate in pranks, albeit mostly of an innocuous nature. His most creative effort was likely his senior year when he successfully impersonated a nonexistent vice principal from the school and was able to have the entire school shut down for a "snow day." The principal learned too late that morning after the local radio station had broadcast the closure. The student body was ecstatic because of the cold inclement weather, including a good bit of snow; also most of the faculty were also pleased with the day off. The principal, a crotchety fellow named Reinhold Heckman wasn't amused. At a later faculty meeting, the consensus was that Will Panzer had been responsible (unproven) for the incident. In trying to understand Will, a few concluded that his behavior was a result of his birth order, that is, the Adlerian idea that the middle child was given less attention and acted out to be noticed. The second idea was that he despised his stepmother as she had usurped the role of his mother. After what seemed endless and fruitless discussion, the varsity basketball coach who rather admired Will, remarked "I think you're all wrong. What we see is the genetics of his ancestry; it's the last remnants of his Teutonic Warrior genes, like Herman the German (Arminius) up on the hill in New Ulm."

Will barely scraped through high school graduating with a C- average, although he did have one major accomplishment in the four years. Oddly, and out of character for Will, he took typing and became highly proficient. In general, however, he didn't give much attention to academics, instead spending his free time pheasant hunting, organizing pranks, drinking alcohol illegally and chasing girls.

Will's family was often exasperated with his continuing shenanigans. His older brother Gunther (the apple of his father's eye and class valedictorian) asked Will, "why is it you always find trouble?"

Will responded, "that's not true, it's the devil's doing."

"What do you mean the devil's doing?"

"Well I'm minding my own business and old Satan sneaks up behind me and bites me in the ass."

"Oh baloney."

"No Gunther, it's a fact."

If in fact some of Will's behavior was the work of the devil, a climatic incident on a hot and muggy June day was likely old Satan's masterpice for the year.

The weather in southern Minnesota in June can really get ugly and when Will got up that morning he knew it was going to be miserable. Then, to make matters worse, his father told Will he wanted him to bale hay, as he and Gunther were going to a machinery auction in Minneapolis. Will was really pissed off; the worst possible job this time of year, with a weather forecast of 85° and the humidity even higher.

However when his father told him who would be helping him, driving the baler, his mood changed immediately. Rachel Fluegel, the daughter of a neighboring farmer, told Will's father she was available to help. Rachel was an eighteen year old girl who had also just graduated from St. Mark's high school and her family attended the same church as the Panzers. All the local young guys described Rachel as being "built like a brick shit house." She really was a knockout, a good German girl with big blue eyes, honey blonde hair, a very athletic build, but best of all she had fabulous "hooters!"

Everyone called her a "tomboy," and she was an unabashed flirt.

About 10:00 AM Rachel showed up and Will wondered how he was going to pay attention to his job. She was wearing a floppy straw hat and a skimpy string halter that barely covered those heavenly creations that God really got right. He couldn't help looking directly at her cleavage and of course when he looked up at her she was grinning (he thought a bit wickedly) and likely knew that he was leering at her.

He could hardly wait to get going just to be alone with her. Little did he understand how this day would dramatically alter the trajectory of his life.

After six hours of miserable grueling heat, near to exhaustion, Will had a brilliant flash.

He asked, "hey Rachel do you have to go home right away?"

"No, I'm in no hurry, what do you have in mind?"

"What do you think about heading for the river and having a nice cool swim?"

"That really sounds great, I'm about half cooked, that water will really feel good."

"Let's unhook the baler and drive there, it's only about a mile."

Will drove the tractor and Rachel stood behind him on the draw bar with her magnificent breasts pressing against his back. Every time they hit a bump those wondeful feminine attributes bounced, causing a titillating electrical charge throughout his system. By the time they reached the creek his manhood was in such a state of arousal he was embarrassed and immediately dove into the water. Rachel followed him, grabbed his head and dunked him underwater.

"Okay Rachel you asked for it," as he lunged across the pool and dunked her.

That started an all out battle with both jumping on one another and repeatedly dunking each other. Suddenly the roughhouse play took on a new dimension; Will realized he was breathing heavily, almost panting. He moved behind Rachel and accidentally (maybe) grasped one of her breasts. Rachel didn't attempt to move away or remove his hand and he realized that she was also becoming aroused.

They swam to a sandbar, literally ripped off their clothes and began a frantic sexual encounter. Will reached orgasm in what he thought might be world record time; later he wondered if they kept statistics on that kind of thing.

After Rachel left for home, Will thought about the encounter; it was exhilarating and he felt no guilt, after all it was Rachel who mostly initiated the encounter. He rationalized, thinking to himself, 'see Gunther trouble comes to me I don't look for it.'

With his youthful history of orchestrating pranks and shenanigans he had often escaped most of the consequences of his behavior. However, the result of Will's idea for a swim in the creek had a far different outcome; Rachel had become pregnant. She was eventually sent to a private facility in Minneapolis to await the birth of the child who would be adopted.

On this occasion Will's father (Heinrich) advised him he would receive full credit for this frenzied frolic with Rachel in the Watonwan River, as it was named. His father also informed Will that he would be volunteering for the United States army later that fall of 1966. After completing basic training he was posted to Vietnam.

DAVID SON OF ISRAEL

Israel: 1950-1977

David and Naomi arrived at Gan Shumel kibbutz in northern Israel, Haifa district, in the spring of 1950 when David was three years old. Even with the loss of his legs (polio) he adapted readily to their new home, making friends immediately and amazing everyone with his ability to ambulate with crutches. Because of his obvious intelligence he was placed in the kindergarten school for children, ages four to seven, even though he was only three.

In the following years he continued his schooling at the kibbutz, finishing high school in 1963 at the age of sixteen. He had a voracious appetite for learning and during the period he mastered most of the curriculums at Gan Shumel. Additionally he participated in any nonacademic activities he could, including plays, debates and contests of knowledge.

One of his teachers at the school had a violin; after much pestering by the rambunctious youth to play it, he ageed to allow David a try. Within six months, much to the surprise and delight of the teacher, he was remarkably proficient.

One evening at a musical concert given by the students, a wealthy elderly gentleman attended and paid particular attention to David playing the violin. He was greatly impressed with David's ability to play, but also was more than a bit enthralled with Naomi, who at forty-nine, was still a regal beauty.

The man, Shimon Cohen sponsored them so they could move to Haifa where David enrolled in the University. He was not completely satisfied at Haifa and after two years he left school doing odd jobs for the next several years.

When he was twenty David transferred to Tel Aviv University where he majored in international relations (intelligence) with minors in law and music (violin). He graduated in 1969 at age twenty-two and taught music for two years in local secondary schools.

Once again he returned to Tel Aviv University, the Buchmann-Metha school of music, (David and Yolanda faculty of the arts), and continued studies in classical violin. By 1974, with appearances throughout Israel, he was being hailed by some as a violin virtuoso. That same year, 1974, at a ceremony honoring newly elected Prime Minister, Itzhak Rabin, David was a featured violinist. Also attending that ceremony was the future Prime Minister Menachem Begin. Begin was so enthralled with the performance that he asked to meet David. That meeting would begin what was to be come a strong friendship between the two men. Over the next three years, Begin came to fully appreciate David's ability as a musician and also his superior intellectual skills. He especially noted David's powers of observation and seeming intuitive nature, to decipher others hidden agendas; ablities that apparently had their genesis when he was a child.

It was also no secret that Menachem Begin had become a great fan of David as a violinist after he first heard him perform in 1974. But it was two events in the next three years, when

Yitzak Rabin was prime minister, that would forever alter the course of David's life, in particular his relationship with Begin.

David was living in Tel Aviv, teaching at the University and tutoring young people who demonstrated exceptional talent in music. He loved his students as he watched them begin to flourish under his guidance. His teaching techniques were an extension of David's character and how he lived his life on a daily basis. He was a creature of habit and paid careful attention to detail. In listening to his students practicing their lessons he caught even the slightest miscue in the melody of the compsition.

His ability to notice even minute mistakes in listening to music carried over to other aspects of his life as he readily detected small or unusal changes in the enviornment around him. He admitted to friends that interpreting (they said guessing) the meanings of unusual or differing visual and auditory observations had become a daily habit. He especially enjoyed watching people, trying to decipher their moods; carefully noting their attire, their manner of walking, if they carried handbags, grocery bags, or other accessories. He was especially interested in (he never understood the reason) how an individual behaved as part of a larger group; did they readily interact with others around them, remain aloof (tend to isolate), stay essentilly in one location, or tend to roam.

Often, after observing an individual, he would then rapidly assemble a mental profile and attempt to predict something about the individual; profession, interests, intelligence and even intentions for the day. Clearly, he rarely discovered the validity of his observations and asumptions, until one fateful day.

His day usually began in the morning with lessons for his students; then around 11:30 AM he headed for his favorite restaurant, Bar Ochel (cheap eats). He most times used a wheelchair for ambulation, but for the short distance to the bus he walked using crutches and long leg braces. Although he struggled the excercise was good for him.

One morning at the stop he observed a slim young man who was also frequently at the loccation. Suddenly he was taken aback (recalling images in his powerful memory bank) as he realized the fellow's appearance had dramatically changed each time he arrived. His style of clothing varied from shorts to long pants, sweaters vs. shirts, differing hats and then no hat. Most interestingly, however, was that he sometimes wore glasses, then no glasses, occasionally sunglasses, and then no glasses of any kind. David's hair bristled on the back of his neck. In the ensuing days he carefully watched the fellow who appeared each day David was there. Every morning the fellow boarded the bus and then would disembark at the popular crowded restaurant that David and dozens of mostly young students and professionals frequented.

A few days later David experienced a sudden dreadful sense of urgency and contacted his friend Menachem Begin, the soon to be prime minister of Israel. They met the following day and David explained his fears in detail. That same day agents from Mossad were assigned surveillance for that bus stop. Within days, on a balmy warm morning the man in question arrived wearing a heavy overcoat, dark sunglasses, a hat, and a newly acquired mustache. David and agents immediately feared what was about to occur. As the bus approached, agents rushed the suspect, grasping his arms and legs, pinning him to the ground. Carefully removing his heavy coat revealed a deadly explosive vest that would likely have killed all or most of the people on the bus. The heroic actions of the man who foiled the bomber was reported throughout Israel, the Middle East and internationally. However, David landau's name was not mentioned in any of the reports.

Several weeks later David again observed an individual, a

young woman, who he noted was present each day he was at the restaurant for lunch. Alarmingly, he realized she was also radically changing her dress and appearance on each visit. He also detected what he interpreted as a high level of stress or anxiety accompanied by a tendency to abruptly leave (almost flee) the premises. Again he alerted Begin and Mossad agents were placed both inside and outside of the restaurant. Within a week the young woman was spotted getting off the bus heading for the restaurant. Initially it was a newly acquired limp that was the immediate cause for alarm. She was attired in a long gown, and her visible apparent pregnancy did not carry life, rather it bore death. The agents called for her to stop and when she began to run they opened fire with automatic weapons. With the initial barrage of gunfire from the 9mm Berettas, the bomb she was carrying detonated showering the area with lethal metal fragments. Anyone in close proimity was spattered with sticky red gore that only moments before had been the flesh, bones and brains of the lone assassin. Miraculously no intended victims were killed, although some suffered significant injuries, with a number being life threatening.

Later that year, July of 1977, when Menachem Begin had been elected premier, he summoned David to meet with himself and the director of Mossad, Yitzhak Hofi.

At that meeting David was asked to accept a position with the internal security unit Shinbat (known in Hebrew as Shabak). He was initially reluctant and tried to dissuade Begin and Hofi. However, after he was assured that only the prime minister, director of Mossad and a limited number of senior members of the agency would know his appointment, he agreed.

MATURATION-THE SEEDS Of HATE

Ishmael: 1967

It was to be a special day for Ishmael, June fifth, 1967; a beautful summer morning in the Siani. He and his parents, Susan and Gamel, had just begun their mornig meal at the Bir Gifgafa airfield. What an occasion! They had been encouraged by president Nasser himself to visit the facility and see how prepared they were to respond to any Israeli aggression.

Several weeks earlier Nasser meeting with EAF Pilots and commanders at a highly publicized event had announced his intentions to close the Straits of Tiran to Israeli shipping. He had said, "we are now on the verge of confrontation with Israel; he added "the Jews threaten us with war? I say to them, "welcome we are ready for war!"

And what a glorious sight here on the airfield with all of the planes ready and waiting to respond to the Israelis and rain destruction upon those infidels. Today, Ishmael thought 'I am especially proud of my Muslim and Egyptian heritage.'

His father started to ask Ishmael a question, he said "Ishmael what do you think....?" And then a blinding flash and tremendous explosion rocked the dining room, knocking over tables and chairs.

His mother screamed, "In the name of Allah what is going on?"

The explosions began to come, one after the other, it seemed the earth was exploding. Windows in the hall began to shatter showering glass throughout the room. Ishmael's father said "get down on the floor; we are being bombed and I have a terrible feeling I know who's doing it."

The explosions were incessant, coming in ever increasing numbers. Gamel stood up and looked out to the airfield and cried, "our planes, our planes, they are all being destroyed, it has to be those damn Jews; where are our fighters, our MIGS, why don't they respond?"

He suddenly bolted to the front door. Susan shrieked, "Gamel, Gamel come back, stay away from the door, you will be killed." He ran out onto the airfield looking at the skies, standing, as if frozen in place.

"I knew it, I knew it, those sons of whores and cur dogs it's the Israelis, the bastards! I can see the planes, Dassault Mirages and the MD 350 Ouragon; dozens of them, like wasps or more like filthy flies swarming overhead."

The building suddenly rocked violently as a missle made a direct hit on the back of the facility. Smoke and dust filled the air choking everyone and causing increased hysteria among the confused and terrified patrons.

"Come on Ishmael and Susan were getting out of here before we're blown to bits."

"Wait father how can we get away, don't you think our vehicle has been destroyed?"

"Well I don't know, but I'm not going to stay here and be killed by filthy pigs from Israel."

They gathered themselves and stumbled out of the building,

now beginning to burn, fueled by ruptured gas lines.

"Get to the Land Rover," Gamel yelled, at least if we get off of the airfield our chances of surviving are better." The vehicle was intact and they clambered aboard with bombs and guided missiles continuing to rain from the skies. Gamel started the vehicle and began to move, then Susan cried, "oh dear I left my purse under the table and it contains all of our money and my jewelry; can't we go get it?"

"No" father said, "let it go, it's not that important."

"Oh no, it's got all of my favorite pieces of jewelry that I brought along for this occasion; please can we get it?"

Ishmael said "I'll do it, it'll only take a second." As Gamel pulled away from the building he yelled, "I'm afraid of gas explosions." Ishmael jumped out of the vehicle raced back to the building, (now in utter chaos), and quickly located his mother's purse covered with dust. He grabbed the purse and raced out of the building onto the tarmac. His father had pulled some distance away and Ishmael thought, 'oh no he's sitting completely exposed on the airfield with no other planes near by.' Then he saw it, a small speck arching down from the sky, like a bird; it had a trail of smoke or vapor following. The emission was not from a bird, it was from a missle! Ishmael screamed "get out, get out," but too late, the bird of death, hit the Land Rover and it disintegrated, literally evaporated before him.

He fell to his knees, sobbing uncontrollably. Confused and disoriented, he took a deep breath and swallowed. His insides burned and a foul taste of saliva permeated his mouth as if he had ingested a pill, a bitter pill of hatred. He felt sick, but refused to vomit. He suddenly felt that he was alone. In fact he was, he had lost his mother and father.

Ishmael was rescued from the airfield and taken to a local military hospital. He was physically unhurt, but had suffered severe psychological trauma. With the shock of witnessing his parents being killed, he began to experience new feelings of raw hatred. His mind raged with thoughts of vengeance and deep visceral stabbing sensations engulfed him.

He had come to fully experience and understand hatred beyond the mere intellectual idea of loathing.

In an instant at Bir Gigafa Airfield Ishmael had become a changed child, destined to embark on a lethal and destructive lifelong journey. The seeds of hate had matured and become full flowered.

TASTE OF BLOOD

Ishmael: 1967-1974

In the days and weeks after the tragic death of his parents Ishmael made a remarkable psychological recovery from their loss. His rapid recuperation was likely related to the rigorous physical and intellectual regimens from early childhood provided by his father and elite cadre of tutors and instructors. Equally important, however, may have been his newly acquired desire for revenge; his need for vengeance would become as a beacon guiding his thoughts, feelings and behaviors in the future.

When Ishmael was born his father had named his brother Ahmed as Ishnael's guardian if anything were to happen to both parents. His uncle was a supportive father figure and unlike Gamel he was mild-mannered. However, surprisingly the day Ishmael arrived at the home of Ahmed, Nour, his wife, unlike many Islamic wives, made it clear that she had the authority to make decisions in her household. She immediately served notice on Ishmael that he was number five in the pecking order of the family; she listed the members in order as herself first, then Ahmed, their two children and lastly Ishmael. Their relationship after the first day never improved and by the time he left for college he carried a smoldering dislike for Nour, a mere woman who didn't know her place. He sometimes fantasized how he could dispose of her, but out of respect for Ahmed he never acted on his evil thoughts. But the next seven years with Nour left a deep wound he would carry for a lifetime.

Ahmed continued to support and encourage Ishmael's ever growing athletic prowess, but additionally encouraged other academic interests including music and languages. As in athletics, Ishmael would demonstrate outstanding ability in learning languages and understanding and appreciating music.

In 1973 with the onset of the Yom Kippur war, Ishmael was to learn that Ahmed in fact did share one of his father's most fervent passions – his hatred of the Jews. Both Ishmael and Ahmed were initially encouraged by the course of the war but the conflict ended with Israel effectively winning the war, even though they experienced a psychological loss in a shattering of their formidable reputation of their defense capabilities. The outcome unexpectedly triggered a torrent of venom from the mouth from Ahmed; additionally his outburst further intensified Ishmael's smoldering loathing of the Jews. Later, alone, he raised his head and shouted, "you filthy Jew dogs one day I will repay your treachery 1000 times more; your guts will rot in the sands of the Sinai and the beasts of the desert will devour your carcasses." Strangely, but unrecognized at the time, the war and its aftermath seemed to bring a heightened closeness to his uncle but further distance Ishmael's relationship with Nour.

Ishmael changed dramatically in those years, not only physically (as he grew to full manhood) but also psychologically and emotionally. He began to increasingly view females (he used the term female pejoratively) as weak, untrustworthy and then often overly aggressive. He despised Nour and her feelings were likely the same towards Ishmael.

However, he readily recognized that most young women had a decidedly positive response to him when they met. Their intentions in trying to establish sexual relationships with him were often blatant. He responded to their advances, used them sexually and then casually discarded them as he did with used condoms. But again, although he reveled in his youthful lust, the aftermath left him emotionally drained, with feelings of humiliation and utter loathing for the girls. He also discovered alcohol and chose to ignore the teachings of the prophet, at times drinking himself into a blind stupor.

He was careful and adept at keeping his secular dissipations unknown to Ahmed, but he felt that the devious Nour suspected his after-hours raucous living. However, she never approached him on the matter as apparently she didn't have any evidence.

Now, at a young age he fully embraced a seething hatred of Israel and all Judaism, accompnied by an intense revulsion for women.

Then when Ishmael was nineteen a tragedy struck the family; Nour suddenly disappeared and her body was found in the Nile River a week or so later. No clues were ever discovered to account for her sudden disappearance and death. Ishmael shed no tears for her loss as he had experienced his first taste of blood.

TRANSFORMATION-PFC TO PHD

Will Panzer: 1966-1995

In the late summer of 1966 Will "volunteered" to join the United States Army. After completing his basic training he was posted to Vietnam and initially assigned to a combat unit. Daily witnessing the carnage around him and the high probability of serious injury or being killed, he began systematic efforts to be reassigned to a noncombat unit. Although he was often impulsive and appeared scattered in his behavior, he was also very adept and capable of identifying a goal and developing strategies to reach that objective. Whether by luck or persistence or a combination of both, he eventually did obtain a position as a clerk typist in a non-combat unit; unbelievably it wasn't at military headquarters, rather it was at the U.S. Embassy in Saigon. His fellow soldiers accused him of even bribing general Westmoreland to get the assignment.

Not long after he began his new assignment he met an individual who would dramatically change his life. Her family name was Nguyen and her father was a high-level diplomat. For unknown reasons (uncharactertic of the majority of contemporary Vietnamese) he was enamored with the history of the French in Indochina; that's the reason people said he named his daughter Camille. She was beautiful, energetic, fun loving, and a tease who captured Will's heart the first time he met her. He pursued her relentlessly and they were married in Saigon in 1967.

In January of 1968 the Tet Offensive was unleashed by the Viet Cong. Will feared that his stay might be extended, but again some suggested, that her father's status insured his tour of duty ended.

They returned to southern Minnesota and Will joined his father and older brother in their now thriving dairy business. Happily married and returning to his roots, he initially began to envision the future with Camille, a large number of children, expanding the family's land holdings, and developing a premeir dairy herd in the state of Minnesota.

However, notwithstanding his high hopes and long-term plans, after only a few months back on the farm Will found himself increasingly restless and as he said at "loose ends." Camille was also not happy living the humdrum life of a Midwestern housewife. She began to encourage Will to possibly return to school to pursue a profession; he thought that maybe Camille was right and he should begin looking into colleges.

Then one evening at a local restaurant, a dinner party, with three other couples (former classmates of Will) he made a comment that he thought was rather humorous and not too risqué for a group of adults. After dinner and more than a few drinks, Will, as was often the case, found himself the center of attention responding to an incessant barrage of questions about Vietnam, the war, the people-it seemed endless. One of the group asked "were you ever in Da Nang?" Will, rather flippantly responded, "actually no, but I was in and out of Pun Tang on a number of occasions."

The reaction to the comment was complete silence. Will was surprised as he thought his classmates understood that at times he would say something not completely appropriate. The party ended awkwardly not long after that. Upon returning home Camille remarked, "Will maybe neither you or I belong here anymore; furthermore we're not even welcome."

"You might be right," he agreed.

Although they were both unhappy, Will found it difficult to abandon his hopes for the family farm. He continued to languish for another two years and then made the decision that he must act.

With Camille's encouragement and assistance he began to submit applications to colleges, mostly in Minnesota. As his high school record mostly reflected his inattention to academics he frequently received letters of denial. Again, at Camille's suggestion he visited Mankato State in Southern Minnesota and met with the dean of admissions. The interview went well and in the fall of 1971 he was accepted at the college. After what seemed five long years of study and continuing support from his wife he completed his degree and in 1976 was awarded a Bachelor of Arts. Having achieved academically for the first time in his life, and with a growing sense of his ability to compete at the university level, he applied to the University of Illinois in 1972 for a masters degree program. He had discovered an academic discipline called horticulture and once he was enrolled, he flourished, completing the program in just two years in 1974. Then with increasing confidence, substantially good grades, persistence, and an ability to ingratiate himself to decision makers he was again accepted for doctoral studies at the University of Illinois majoring in horticulture and agricultural engineering. While at Illinois he began to be recognized and acknowledged as an expert in greenhouse construction and food growing systems.

After receiving his degree in 1978 he obtained a teaching position at Rutgers University. He taught there until 1986 and then accepted a position at the University of Arizona, recruited by a man named Kevin O'Connell. He and O'Connell worked well together and became trusted colleagues. He left Arizona for a position at California Polytechnic University in San Luis Obispo in 1990 and finally in 1995 he rejoined Kevin O'Connell at Oregon State University. Like Panzer, who was becoming recognized internationally for his work in controlled environment agriculture and greenhouse construction, O'Connell was also now recognized as an international expert in greenhouse aquaculture, notably tilapia farming.

The transformation of Will Panzer was complete.

Years later, ruminating about the major events in his life that may have impacted on his probable destiny as a "grease monkey" car mechanic to the hallowed halls of academia, he identified three factors.

Clearly his marriage to Camille was instrumental. However, he also concluded that baling hay on a miserably hot June day and proficiency on his old Royal Typewriter were likely a close second and third place.

HAND OF ALLAH

Ishmael: 1975-1992

In 1975 at the age of twenty, Ishmael enrolled in Oxford University to study languages.

Ishmael was a brilliant student as his early education with select tutors and relentless pressure from his father to excel, translated into later outstanding academic success. Invariably, although he finished close to first in all of his studies, intentionally (even a mystery to himself) he ensured that he did not finish at the top of the class. He wasn't sure why, but at one point early in his tenure at Oxford, he experienced what he interpreted as a sign he attributed to the mighty Allah; it was to maintain anonymity, to avoid being recognized or noticed.

Notwithstanding, his academic credentials were superior and he graduated in 1980. Again he had manipulated his semester class schedules to make sure he didn't graduate in four years.

In 1981 he accepted a position in Middle Eastern Studies at the American University of Cairo in Egypt, teaching Arabic as a foreign language (TAFL). A primary motivation was not the teaching or the money, rather the opportunity to meet young women. With his handsome good looks and sensuous charm, he regularly cut a wide swath through the virginity of countless young damsels of the Nile.

However, in 1984, having lived a life of total debauchery for three years, he became bored and abruptly resigned his position and left for Europe. He traveled across the continent, East to West and North to South, once again continuing to maintain a life of excess. For the next two years he wandered, almost aimlessly, throughout the continent with an unwanted companion he labeled as "restlessness" and at times even "despair." In his journeys he could never escape the haunting feelings of his desire for vengeance.

He readily developed positive relationships with people from diverse cultures, as others were readily attracted to his magnetic personality. However, he soon lost interest in his new found friends, invariably again feeling he did not belong.

Then precipitously he decided to explore South America, traversing the continent from the Isthmus of Panama to Tierra del Fuego; he continued to feel restless and aimless. In 1987, after only one year, he again impulsively fled the land of the Amazon and ended up in London, England.

One evening, in early 1988, drinking scotch at the elegant Savoy hotel on the north bank of the Thames River, he encountered a man also drinking his favorite, Craggonmore. He introduced himself to the man named Mustafa Aziz, who was originally from Palestine.

They began a casual conversation and soon both well fortfied with the excellent highland whisky, discovered they had much in common. They were both Islamic, but not practicing the tenets at this time, unencumbered by marriage, and essentially living a hedonistic lifestyle. Most importantly however, Mustafa was also violently anti-Israeli. That first encounter was extremely gratifying for both men and led to continuing meetings for drinks and discussions of world affairs. Mustafa was also highly educated and although they covered a diverse variety of subjects, invariably their discussions seemed to eventually focus on Israel.

Mustafa owned an import- export business in San Francisco, California and had recently opened an office in Kuala Lumpur, Malaysia. Eventually Mustafa asked Ishmael about his interest in his growing company. Although Ishmael was somewhat intrigued with the idea he was non-commital, but did maintain contact with Mustafa during the ensuing year.

One evening drinking Craggonmore alone he inadvertently finished a full quart of the fine whisky; in a stupor, he stumbled into bed. The entire night was filled with bizarre and at times frightening dreams. One vivid image of his semi-conscious sleep was of himself at a young age in the Tahfiz school in Malaysia memorizing verses of the Quran. In the dream it was a happy time and a period of joyful learning. He awoke and sat silently contemplating the meaning of his dream. After more than two hours of thinking an answer came to him; reverently he said softly, "yes I understand, it is Allah admonishing me to return to the place where I first fully understood and embraced my Islamic faith."

Later that day he contacted Mustafa and accepted a position with his company. One condition of his acceptance was that he eventually be posted to the office in Kuala Lumpur.

It was 1990 when he began working with the company and for next two years he shuttled between San Francisco and Kuala Lumpur. Then in 1992 he was permanently transferred to Kuala Lumpur to manage the operations of the company. Unknown to Ishmael at the time, the move was to preordaine his future destiny.

THE TWIN

Kuala Lumpur: 1995

It was a sweltering evening in Kuala Lumpur. In fact, from October to December most days are hot and steamy and the only escape is air conditioning indoors.

Ishmael Abboud had retreated into the sanctuary of a restaurant-bar that someone suggested served excellent cuisine. It was named Johnny's place for an American expatriate from the Vietnam War who had decided not to return to America when the conflict ended.

He had never frequented the establishment and was taken aback when the bartender said "well hello Terry, you're a bit early this evening."

"I'm sorry," Ishmael replied, "who did you say I was?"

"Terry, Terry Fitzroy of course; Terry have you developed amnesia?"

"Sir, I can assure you I am not someone named Terry Fitzroy, my name is Ishmael."

"My god man you look exactly Like Terry. I'D have bet a fistful of ringgit's that you were Terry."

"My apologies to disappoint you, but I am not the person you named; did you say Terry?"

The bartender perked up and said "tell you what he's here almost every day, I'll bring him over to see you when he comes in."

Ishmael removed his sunglasses, and stared intently at him.

"No my good man don't do that. If I wish to meet this Terry I prefer an intoduction on my terms; furthermore I would appreciate you not mentioning me to this fellow."

"Sir you don't," but Ishmael interrupted.

"Now I know you mean well, but I really don't want to meet this Terry; so drop the matter."

The bartender was a bit shaken as the stranger was seemingly being polite, but the ferocity in his eyes was chilling. He said no more.

"I am going to take a table in the back, order dinner, and do some reading. Have my drinks sent back to me."

Ishmael had dinner and when he finished eating he began to read. He also carefully watched as each patron entered the bar. An hour or so later he glanced up as a man entered the front door. As the fellow turned to face the bar, showing the full profile of the his face, Ishmael gasped and whispered to himself, "in the name of Allah I must be hallucinating, that man is me." He thought, 'I can't believe, it he could be my brother, no my twin;. no wonder the bartender thought I was that guy.'

The newcomer was obviously well known, greeting not only the bartender, but also other individuals seated at the bar. Ishmael suddenly felt ill at ease, he slouched in his chair, put on his sunglasses, and lifted his newspaper in front of his face. He was unsure of his reaction. All of his senses, mental and physical, seemed to be highly stimulated and he realized his hands were shaking. In a few moments he relaxed somewhat and sat quietly for a time. He lowered the newspaper to again glance at his look-alike. He thought 'it's uncanny how closely he resembles me. I wonder who he is? I guess he's a half-breed like me, brown and white; what a shock'. It was indeed a shock and he could not dispel his feelings of uneasiness.

Ishmael had several more drinks, occasionally glancing at the fellow named Terry. Then he left through the rear entrance, avoiding an encounter with the unknown man.

In the ensuing days he frequently found himself thinking of the man at the bar. The memory of the fellow began to invade his thinking on a daily basis and Ishmael began to feel frustrated and even stressed. One evening when the recurring memory reached a flashpoint, he cried aloud "why in the name of Allah can't I forget the bastard, whoever he is?" On these occasions he usually poured himself several shots of his favorite single malt scotch whisky. With his senses numbing he would relax and began attempting to understand his almost obsession with the stranger. 'I wonder', he thought, 'is continually returning to thinking about this man some kind of sign for me? Could it be that the all powerful one is trying to tell me that this "twin" is part of his plan for me?' Ishmael also found himself increasingly restless and at times uninterested in his export business, trips to Johnny's, and life in general.

Then one morning, in early 1995, having coffee and reading the local newspaper, he noted an article concerning a free lecture by an American named Dr. Kevin O'Connell. O'Connell was on a six month sabbatical lecture tour under a Fulbright visiting professors program to the Asian Institute of Technology in Bangkok, Thailand. He had been invited by the Indonesian government to present a series of lectures on aquaculture, with a focus on tilapia fish farming. 'Why not' thought Ishmael 'I have nothing better to do.' He did attend the lecture early the following evening and although the topic was only mildly interesting, several other bits of information that O'Connell casually shared caught Ishmael's full attention. O'Connell had mentioned that Oregon State University, his employer, was strongly committed to increasing the number of international students enrolling at their institution, including individuals from Asian countries. He also mentioned, underscoring this commitment, in the near future OSU would begin advertising for a newly created position to achieve these goals. O'Connell also made a few brief remarks concerning a proposed international tilapia project between the United States and Israel. The mention of the joint Israel/USA project sent a charge of energy, literally a shock, throughout Ishmael's body.

He listened carefully to the remainder of the lecture taking notes in detail on everything O'Connell presented. He was tempted to ask questions, but intuitively remained silent.

Returning home he fixed himself a triple shot of scotch attempting to quell chaotic sensations of agitation and then exhilaration throughout his entire system.

"What's wrong with the," he uttered aloud, "why am I feeling this way" he fretted. When the alcohol accomplished its intent, he relaxed and fell into a fitful sleep.

When he awoke early the next morning he felt a sense of release from the earlier mental and physical tension. He sat up in bed and exclaimed loudly, "yes, it is truly Allah who is guiding me; first to this man Terry and then to hear O'Connell's lecture. They must hold keys to my future." Later, he began to think more about his revelation that morning. He wondered if he had been singled out as a special messenger to carry out the wishes of the almighty one. Even though he had knowingly violated many of the tenets of Islam, he also knew that Allah was a merciful and forgiving God. Had he been given a holy dispensation which allowed him to follow pleasurable paths, but also steps that would lead to the destruction of his personal enemies and those of Islam? He thought, 'I am not sure the direction I must take, but with Allah leading me, I will find the way.'

TERENCE FITZROY-THE PAWN

Kuala Lumpur: 1995

After ten days of contemplating what action to take concerning the man named Terry, he returned to Johnny's bar. However, this time he went in search of the man who could have been his twin.

When he entered the bartender again started with "well hello," and then stopped and said "I'm sorry man, I really can't tell who you are; I don't want to call you Terry if you are not him."

Ishmael smiled and said "hey no problem and I'm not the guy you know as Terry."

"Yes, I'm sorry that I thought you were Terry Fitzroy."

"Well for the record my name is Ishmael and I have to admit that my curiosity has gotten the best of me."

Ishmael was thinking that he might need to salve any wounds that he had caused with his initial encounter with the bar man.

"I'm a little pissed off at myself for behaving rather badly when you mistook me for this fellow Terry; might I apologize to you and we can start over with no hard feelings?"

Ishmael's demeanor was sincere and convincing and he could sense that the bartender was completely accepting his initiative.

"No, there is no problem at all; I guess I did jump on your ass the instant you walked in the door. How about a drink on me and we call it even?"

"Sounds good to me, I'll have a scotch, single malt."

"Would you like one of the classics?"

"Sure, do you have Cragganmore?"

"Of course, but I also carry the others, at least what I think are the classics. Oban, Lagavulan, etc.. Have you ever tried all of them?"

"No, I haven't; as a matter of fact maybe I will try the Lagavulan."

"Good choice; it has an oily smoky peat aroma. Some say it's synonymous with the Islay signature peat."

Ishmael ordered a second round, this time Cragganmore. Then he surprised the bartender saying, "Johnny, tell you what, if that fellow Terry comes in, bring him over to meet me."

"Well Ishmael I'm happy to hear you say that; Terry is really a nice guy. He's kind of shy and I'm not sure how many friends he has as he's kind of a loner. However, I think he's a really intelligent guy. I think he is a graduate of Cambridge."

Ishmael found a table and waited; within the hour Terry walked in. Johnny greeted him, pointed to Ishmael, and then led him towards the table. When Terry got close to Ishmael he stopped, wide- eyed, and then turned pale. Ishmael stood, reached out his hand and said "well you really do look like me. Hah!" Terry continued to gaze at Ishmael and finally stammered, "unbeliveable, I can't believe there is another me on this planet."

"Oh, not another you, but we sure do resemble each other.

Have a seat, would you care for a drink?"

"Yes, thanks; I'm a bit flabbergasted at seeing you."

They proceeded to have several drinks together, mostly exchanging information about their work. Terry operated a bookstore and gift shop and Ishmael told him he owned an import/export business. Early on Ishmael guessed that Terry was gay; a lifestyle that Ishmael viewed as deviant and disgusting. However, after leaving the bar, he was mystified by not feeling repulsed or annoyed with the man. Once again he rationalized believing that he was being guided by Allah towards an unknown objective. Before they left the bar Terry asked if Ishmael would be coming back to Johnny's. Without hesitation Ishmael replied "yes I'll be here again."

It had been October when Ishmael had intially gone to Johnny's and over the next several months he regularly frequented the bar, and invariably he was joined by Terry. Ishmael tolerated him and had become aware that Terry was developing much more than a casual relationship with him. One evening Ishmael decided to seek more information about this man. Terry said his father was English and his mother had come from India. Ishmael wanted the details of his life, which Terry was more than willing to share. Ishmael recognized Terry not only wanted to tell him about his life but was very pleased that he had been asked. Ishmael made sure they were both well lubricated with their favorite scotch, guessing that Terry would be very forthcoming about his life-and he was.

"Ishmael, what about you? I know nothing of you only that you enjoy good scotch!"

"No Terry, it's your turn first, we can get to my squalid past later."

"OK, were should I start?"

"Anywhere you feel comfortable."

"As you know already I'm English, at least fifty percent.

My mother was an Indian princess; her name was Kanti which means beauty and she was indeed beautiful."

"What do you mean by saying she was a princess?"

"Do you really want to know?"

"Try me."

"OK here goes. In 1904 a Hindu Raj named Nilmoni Singha passed away. He was the sixtieth and last king of Mallabhum from the Bengal area. He had at least two wives, maybe more and Kalipada Singha Thakur was the grandson of the second wife named Prasannyamoyee."

"Wait a minute Terry, I didn't ask for a lecture on Indian history."

"Ishmael my mother was a descendant of that guy."

"OK, I understand, but how did your father fit into that family?"

"My father's father, Geoffrey Fitzroy had a tea plantation in Darjelling, West Bengal. Old Geoffrey apparently died young, I don't know the date. They said he drank too much gin and that's what killed him. My father, Malcolm, was born in 1920 and legally inherited the plantation in 1930. The old man, Geoffrey, had become acquainted with the Raj and later my father also came to know the family. In 1952 he married my mother Kanti and I came along in 1955."

"Terry that's quite a story; what did your father do professionally?"

"Really nothing else but live off the income from the plantation which was very substantial. Oh, he was also quite shrewd and invested heavily in securities and bonds; I guess he really made a killing."

"Where are your parents now?"

"They are both gone. They loved to travel and unfortunately on an extended vacation in South America they were both killed in a small plane crash in Brazil in 1987."

"I am sorry to hear that."

"Well, we were estranged and I hadn't seen or spoken with them for four or five years."

"Really, what was that all about?"

"It's related to who I am as a person and choices I have made in my life; I'd like to wait until another time to get into that if you don't mind."

"No, of course not, another day is fine."

They parted company and Ishmael returned home. He mixed a potent scotch and soda and began to rethink about his conversation with Terry. Relaxing he began to experience a growing sense of elation. He murmured aloud, "yes it is surely Allah who is leading me." Ishmael began to visualize the beginnings of a complex scheme that would ultimately lead to the fruition of his evil intentions.

He thought, 'the mist is lifting and the horizon is becoming clear.' And as the dawn drives away the darkness, by morning so had Ishmael's destiny been illuminated by the morning sun.

'Now I must act carefully,' he thought to himself, as though to verbalize the words could somehow expose his diabolic scheming.

Ishmael Abboud at the age of forty had indeed become a man who felt he had few equals. In fact he was highly intelligent, articulate, forceful in action and decision-making; also handsome, likable, charming, and especially persuasive. Holding the belief, as an anointed messenger of Allah, he believed he would ultimately prevail in all that he pursued.

However along with these positive characteristics he was ruthless, vicious, seemingly without a conscience, and full of hatred and vengeance. Without question he was arguably one of the most dangerous and deadly individuals one might encounter.

AMSTERDAM AMBUSH

Will Panzer/Kevin O'Connell: 1988

In 1986 Dr. Kevin O'Connell had developed a major tilapia aquaculture project at the University of Arizona in Tucson. In two short years after completing his doctoral degree, Kevin had achieved national recognition for his specialization in greenhouse aquaculture.

That same year he hired Dr. Will Panzer, who was also recognized for his expertise in greenhouse construction and growing systems. With O'Connell's background in aquaculture and Panzer's strengths in facilities and systems, they felt the combination of knowledge and experience would result in an outstanding team for development of their programs.

Undoubtedly Panzer was likely the most qualified and therefore leading candidate for the position. However, in addition to Panzer's obvious qualifications for the job, a little known event in the past may have also had an impact on O'Connell's decision to hire Panzer. Other professional colleagues who were aware of the incident would suggest that in El Salvador (1985) O'Connell discovered a risk-taking soul mate and wanted him on his team.

Kevin O'Connell was born in Key West Florida in 1950, the oldest of three children. He attended a local grade school in Key West and graduated from high school in Homestead Florida in 1968. The high school was heavily multicultural with American black children, Haitians, Cubans, students from other Caribbean countries and a variety of ethnically diverse Anglos. The diversity of the school was to have a lasting positive impact on Kevin in his later interactions with internationals from differing countries.

After graduation he worked for his father who owned a successful charter fishing business. As the oldest son, his father planned for him to take over operations when he retired. While working in the charter business, Kevin also attended West Florida University and after eight long tiring years of schooling and work he received a B.S. degree in marine biology in 1976.

After receiving his degree he told his father, "I have lived in Florida my entire life and before I settle down here I want to see more of the world; particularly the west and maybe Mexico." He left Florida and essentialy spent the next three years doing odd jobs and in his words, bumming. He went West to Arizona, spent another year in South America and then into Mexico.

At Puerto Penasco Mexico, in 1980, he met a hard charging entrepreneur named Carl Hodges, who was director of The Environmental Research Lab at the University of Arizona in Tucson. The ERL had greenhouse and aquaculture projects literally throughout the world. Hodges was astonishingly successful in raising money, negotiating with heads of state, ruling sheik's in the Middle East and billionaire capitalists from America. Kevin, by chance, had heard of an aquaculture shrimp project in this city under the leadership of Hodges. He arranged a visit to the project and would meet a cast of characters both "homegrown" and also international experts; some quite eccentric, a few with tarnished pasts, but without exception, tops in their fields of expertise. After two days of visiting with the staff his future professional aspirations were firmly embedded in his mind.

In 1981 after having spent the past five years of mostly aimless wandering, he enrolled at the University of Arizona. He began a master's program in Ecology and Evolutionary Biology and stayed at the university completing a PHD in aquaculture in 1984. Subsequently he took a position with the university at the Environmental Research lab (ERL).

The initial impression that most people had of Kevin O'Connell was of a reserved, cautious, non- risk taking individual. However, his calm demeanor belied a man who occasionally seemed to knowingly accept professional assignments that had the potential for personal harm.

Two occasions that demonstrated his willingness to venture into potentially dangerous circumstances were a 1983 trip to Medellin Columbia and a subsequent adventure into civil war torn El Salvador in 1987.

In 1983, still a PHD candidate at Arizona, Kevin and another senior staff member from the ERL visited Columbia to evaluate the potential for an aquaculture project. The first day in Medellin, most likely Pablo Escobar's cartel thugs, instigated a gun battle on the street where Kevin and his companion Abe were walking. When the first shots were fired, Abe shrieked "oh no kevin we are dead, what can we do?"

Calmly Kevin replied "no we're not dead yet," and hustled the terrified man into a cantina close to where they were standing.

"OK now what do we do Kevin?"

Kevin replied, "well let's have several Cervezas and then resume our walk when the shooting stops."

In 1985 Will Panzer, then his professional colleague from Rutgers University, and Kevin visited a struggling aquaculture facility in El Salvador during their civil war. The second day of their inspection tour, after a two hour bus ride from the airport, a frightening incident occurred. Around 12:00 noon a dozen heavily armed government troops suddenly burst into the greenhouse, summarily rounded up ten workers and rather violently escorted them away.

Will asked, "what the hell was that all about?"

The greenhouse manager replied, "please senor be quiet, don't ask."

Will persisted, "why did they take those guys? What's going on?"

"The soldiers must think the people they took are (FMLN), Farabundo Marti National Ltberation Front sympathizers."

"What happens now?"

Two days later none of the ten individuals had returned to work and neither Kevin or Will asked any more questions.

That evening, in their sparse living quarters, drinking shots of tequila they decided that Carl Hodges wouldn't mind if they chartered a helicopter back to the airport in lieu of the two hour bus ride.

Neither O'Connell or Panzer ever shared the contents of a later meeting with Hodges concerning the unauthorized "helicopter" caper.

One morning in 1988, over coffee, two years after being hired by kevin at the University of Arizona, Will was reporting to Kevin on the progress he had made in obtaining additional state support for acquiring new greenhouse space. Will had taken the lead in working with the legislature and told Kevin that he had likely identified the key legislator, a fellow by the name of Lester Heavenly, who appeared ready to move forward with their request.

"Heavenly! Is that really his name?"

"Yes I agree it's kind of different."

"I'm not sure I'd ever heard of a surname Heavenly before?"

"Makes me wonder how the devil his parents came up with that name."

"Well actually Heavenly wasn't the original name."

"What do you mean; where did the name come from," asked a puzzled Kevin?

"Old Lester, who happened to be a bishop in the Baptist Church changed his name from Hatfield to Heavenly."

Kevin paused for a moment, then smiled, and started laughing; he muttered, "what, did he want his name to sound more saintly?"

"Well, the problem was with the name Hatfield."

"How do you know that?"

"I have to admit that I sort of steered him into telling me. I took him to lunch and we began to exchange family stories and eventually Lester got to the name Heavenly."

"So what's the story?"

"He told me that when he started preaching people sometimes would jokingly ask him if he was a relative of the infamous Hatfield/Mccoy saga. He said it began to bother him as he was from hill country in Missouri and he didn't want anyone to assume he was related to a bunch of violent hillbillies."

"You have to be kidding."

"No, I'm not, that's what Lester told me. He's very conservative. He rose through the ranks of his church (though I don't really know what that means), got into politics and was elected to the state legislature. He represents a mostly rural constituency and along with his saintly sounding name I'd guess that's how he kept getting elected. He has been returned to office repeatedly and is now chairman of the legislative appropriations committee."

It had taken Will almost a year to finally identify the individual who would move forward with their request, and that person was of course Lester Heavenly.

Will had not only made frequent trips to Phoenix, he also sent Lester vegetables from their greenhouse operations and provided complimentary basketball and football tickets as Lester was a rabid sports fan. Continually providing small gifts and his persistence on each visit detailing the need for additional greenhouse facilities eventually had results. Lester introduced a bill to provide for several new greenhouse structures at a cost of 500-600,000 dollars.

When the bill began to flounder in the committee, Panzer played his "ace in the hole." He first convinced O'Connell and then (an initially reluctant) Heavenly to accompany them to an international horticulture/aquaculture conference in Amsterdam, Holland. Panzer made all of the arrangements and they were off to the tulip capital of the world. Lester, unaccustomed to international travel did find the trip exciting and completely enjoyable. Although Lester did not drink alcohol, his family tradition allowed for medicinal use of spirits. As he occasionally experienced what he termed "sudden onset of acute arthritis" it was permissible to imbibe in therapeutic drinks of brandy. One evening at dinner in Amsterdam with Lester experiencing some discomfort, (he labled acute arthritis), Will coaxed him into trying some of Europe's finest "medicinal cognac" to ease his pain. After more than one cognac Lester was beaming without a single twinge.

With all of them in a jovial mood, how the discussion of Amsterdam's famous "red light district" surfaced was never clarified. Nontheless, after dinner they ventured out to one of the three well known districts, DeWallen (the walls) to see the sights. After several hours Kevin suggested they head back to the hotel. Surprisingly, Lester advised them he wanted to see more of the district and that he would catch a cab later back to the hotel. Lester never shared any of his solo experiences after he left Kevin and Will that evening; however six weeks after returning to Arizona the state legislature appropriated new funding to the University of Arizona for greenhouse construction in the amount of 545,000 dollars!

That would not be the last unconventional methodology utilized by the two free spirits resulting in significant additional funding for their programs.

Will and Kevin parted company in 1990 as Oregon State University was able to lure O'Connell to their emerging tilapia aquaculture program. Kevin had become recognized as one of the leading experts in the field; a long journey from his blue collar family roots.

Panzer would eventually leave Arizona and be reunited with O'Connell at Oregon State in 1995.

Because of their often unorthodox methods in obtaining funding for new programs during their four years together in Arizona, fellow professionals began to refer to them as those two "Arizona Tilapia Cowboys." Their colleagues began to assume that they should expect the unexpected from the twosome. However most would agree that the highlight of their creative shenanigans was obtaining half a million dollars of funding in consort with one Lester Heavenly.

Aruguably their most creative caper, it became known in the Colleege of Agriculture as the "Amsterdam Ambush."

TILAPIA PROJECT-THE GAN

Oregon State University/ ISRAEL: 1997

Before Will Panzer was hired by Oregon State University he and Kevin O'Connell had been discussing the idea of a joint OSU/Israeli Tilapia project to be located in the Negev Desert of Israel. After Panzer arrived in Corvallis they completed the application in conjunction with a team from Israel during the fall of 1996. The project was approved in the fall 1997 with a targeted start date for the spring of 1999. They were elated with the announcement of the approval and decided to meet with university President Manuel Silva to discuss the award.

Will was able to schedule a meeting for the following week as the president was eager to learn the details of this major award. Kevin had the honor of doing the presentation.

"Sir we will begin with an overall description of the project and spend as much time as you want on areas were you would like more detail. If any information seems redundant let me know and I can skip over that material. I should mention that the project has already been named, the Gan, by the Israelis. The word Gan means "garden"; they were adamant concerning the name and we agreed in order to avoid any initial disagreements."

Kevin then began. "The Project will be a five-year grant award between Oregon State University and the country of Israel. Funding was provided by the Jewish National Fund, the US Department of Agriculture, Foreign Ag Service, and the Gates – Buffet Foundation; combined they provide approximately ninety percent of the costs with ten percent funded by private investors. The project is a commercial– research venture and will be located in the Negev area of Israel near the Arava Valley. The physical plant is located on 300 acres (120 hectares) and will include facilities for incubation, growing fish, research, processing equipment, heating/cooling, storage, administrative offices, brood stock grow out, lab, cafeteria, greenhouse, packing shed, restaurant, market and dormitory facilities. The entire facility will be started with diesel power but eventually solar panels will be added and utilization of the shallow low-grade geothermal aquifer. The water is too salty to drink directly, but easily manipulated with distillation to get fresh water for drinking, the fish hatchery and starting vegetables in shade houses.

Staffing:

A. Overall plant manager and site project director.

B. Hatchery manager and assistant.

1. Biologists, engineers, computer specialists (software and hardware).

2. Production manager: grows fish from fingerlings to salable size.

3. Coordinators: for feed mill, production, processing, and laboratory.

4. Hatchery manager: will closely monitor the technology developed by Cuban biologists (extra growth genes) resulting

in double growth hormones.

C. Director of research unit: for personel from Oregon State, Israel, and university students.

D. Director of marketing: works with wholesalers and major restaurants worldwide to develop contracts and distribution schedules.

E. Director of publicity and public relations: will handle publication of newsletters, assist with marketing materials, arrange for tours (particularly for notable guests) and development of related materials.

F. Security director: will supervise four to six armed guards. The entire perimeter of the project will be surrounded with an eight to ten foot razor-wire topped eletric fence with systems to detect any break in the fence.

Project operations:

1. Produce eggs and fish (vertical integration); also for other farms to use.

2. Raise fish to marketable size – (800 to 900 grams).

3. Process and market fish.

4. Institute an ongoing program of research in growing and food systems.

5. Serve as an international training ground for biologists and other specialists in fisheries; specializing in bringing Palestinian and other Arabs to work with the Israelis and others (Europeans, Americans, Africans and Asians).

6. As part of the training function, (5) develop online training conferences regionally and internationally.

7. Offer tours and provide written and video materials upon request.

Growing Systems:

1. Use a combination of circular tanks and rectangular raceways.

2. Use demand feeders where fish bump hanging rods suspended from a fish hopper along with time feeders that use a spinning plate below the hopper.
3. Use belt feeders; the belt winds a clock mechanism, then feed will be placed on the belt which will be dropped into the tanks for ten hours while the belt winds back up on the spool.
4. Use underwater cameras and audio systems to monitor fish activity and feeding.
5. Use effluent waste water from the farm to irrigate fruit trees and vegetables at the complex.

Project location:

The project is located on an abandoned kibbutz that lies some twenty to thirty miles south of Beersheba in the northern region of the Negev. The whole operation is run on a shallow salty geothermal aquifer.

Budget:

1. Start up costs are five to ten million dollars (US); project directors will have discretion for expenditures up to 10,000. Competitive bids required above 10,000.
2. Annual operating costs will be three to four million; again with directors having discretion for expenditures up to 10,000. Competitive bids required above 10,000.

International advisory committee:

At this time the formation of the committee is still under deliberation. I'm guessing there will be some issues related to the more nationalistic representatives from Israel. Don't quote me on that, but I think eventually they will get it worked out. Of course President Silva you will serve ex officio. Also the Israeli prime minister or his designee will also serve in that capacity."

Kevin paused, and then asked, "President Silva is that

enough detail?"

"Yes, I think so, that's great information; my goodness this is really a comprehensive project. Let me be the first to congratulate you on this outstanding achievement. Having said that, I know of course many others, particularly your fellow professionals are applauding your creative abilities in bringing this project to fruition. I really do look forward to the day I can visit the project."

Will commented, "I agree, when I first had a look at the entire scope of the program I was very impressed. Concerning the project President Silva, I think it's important to note that while many people were involved in the development, Kevin really was the key individual bringing the concept into being. He used his connections to bring together a partnership to demonstrate that an integrated farming project could be developed in one of the harshest deserts in the world; requiring minimal outside resources and resulting in no damage to the surrounding environment."

"Thanks Will, but many people, and specifially you, had major input formulating the project. I would also like to add that the project can also be seen as a social initative. It will bring together Arabs and Israelis, Americans and Iranians, Europeans and Middle Eastern immigrants, along with East Asians to work cooperatively together. Additionally their initiatives will develop technologies that each can take back to their home countries. Finally, one of the major benefits of the diversity of the participants will result in a new appreciation for people traditionally feared and misunderstood at home."

President Silva remarked, "Once again, many thanks to the three of you for taking time to outline the project. Now, although you didn't provide any input I know you're the new fellow in the International Students Office, isn't that correct?"

"Yes, Terry Fitzroy is the name and as you know I'm very

interested in all of our international programing initiatives.”

“Yes, good to meet you Terry. OK gentlemen, if there's nothing else I think that concludes the briefing.”

They all left in an upbeat mood except for one person. Terry thought to himself, 'what a bunch of bullshit. They think the project is going to make everyone great friends and all of the years of hostilities will magically disappear. I and others with the help of the almighty one, Allah, will one day bring about very differing results.'

MENACHEM ALLON

Gan Project Director: 1997

"As to the question ladies and gentlemen, while I understand the basis of the inquiry, in my view the idea is simply ludicrous. I don't mean to sound harsh, but investing authority in an individual to provide leadership and at the same time proposing decision-making be on the basis of a committee is to send the endeavor on the road to perdition. Maybe I should have simply said an unequivocal no!"

Menachem Allon, who was being interviewed for the position of overall director of the joint Oregon State/Israeli Tilapia project (the Gan), had responded emphatically to the question from a member of the interviewing committee. The query concerned Menachem's thoughts on sharing the position with a co-director or even a three person triad.

"I think back to ancient Rome and the First Triumvirate of three powerful ruthless men, Caesar, Pompey and Crassus, who likely only came together to guard their interests against the other two. If your desire is for a single person in a leadership position then I'm interested, otherwise I wouldn't accept an offer."

Selecting the director of the project was not only controversial for some members of the committee, longer term it left some wounded egos. The difficulty arose from the background of the eventual person hired for the position, Menachem Allon. He was a decorated hero of the Yom Kippur war of 1973. As a twenty-eight-year-old brilliant tank commander, he had entered the conflict as a captain and at the completion of the hostilities had emerged with an unprecedented promotion to full colonel. He was an avowed nationalist which concerned some who viewed the project as an opportunity for lessening Mideast tensions and developing new relationships among diverse groups. Furthermore, his lineage was another problem because of his father Levi. Born in 1910, Levi was a former colonel in the Irgun, which he had joined in 1932. Irgun was a Zionist paramilitary organization in the Palestine Mandate, during the period 1920-1948. They had broken away from Haganah, the main paramilitary organization of the Jewish population (Yishuv) during that time. Because they were so much more militant, multiple international groups labeled them a terrorist organization.

Additionally, Menachem was named after Menachem Begin the last commander of Irgun and the Prime Minister of Israel from 1977 to 1983.

Levi, his father had started a homegrown tilapia aquaculture business in late 1980. After a highly successful career with an exporting company in Jerusalem as their CEO, Menachem joined his father and two brothers in their venture. He soon assumed leadership for the project which thrived under his direction.

Based on his demonstrated leadership in the Yom Kippur war, his substantial resume in corporate Israel and his father's tilapia business along with what many would call his charismatic persona, he appeared to be a strong candidate for the position. He had an imposing physical appearance, standing 6'2' tall, described as handsome, with a quiet demeanor, quick to smile and one who loved humor. These characteristics however tended to mask his type A personality, an intense drive for perfection, and the ability for decisive decision-making.

Kevin O'Connell, one of the authors of the project did have concerns with Menachem's often seemingly unbending commitment to the ideals and support of his Israeli homeland. One of Kevin's underlying objectives for the project was the opportunity to demonstrate how the program could forge new relationships and lead to conciliation among previously distrustful groups.

Kevin had said, "Menachem, you know that this project is more than just raising fish. We want to demonstrate, literally to the entire world, that people of good will, regardless of past circumstances and animosities, given the opportunity, can overcome history and become trusted partners for the future. Your dedication to your homeland is well known and your actions in defense of your country are almost legendary. Those are all admirable characteristics that you have demonstrated; the sixties and seventies are not that far away in history and I would not want any of the issues of that time to impact on this project and your ability to lead. I hope you understand what I'm trying to say; I'm not suggesting that you couldn't set aside the past, however, there may be some who come to work on this project who still retain residual difficulties, maybe even grievances. As the project director you could be confronted with those attitudes and would need to be able to handle them."

Menachem nodded differentially to Kevin as a knowing smile crossed his face. He said, "Dr. O'Connell, I appreciate those thoughts, they are very appropriate. It is true I am a strong Israeli nationalist. I love my country and have answered the call to defend them in their time of need. I am a student of history having lived in the Mideast all my life; I do understand the issues and feelings that many other diverse groups in this land have concerning their homelands. There have been many tragedies perpetrated by differing groups and countries over the past decades. There have also been many initiatives attempting to resolve often centuries-old differences. I do understand what you hope to accomplish with this project and I support those objectives. As you know my namesake is Menachem Begin, former Prime Minister of Israel who at one time was the last commander of the Jewish paramilitary organization known as Irgun. It was born of the ashes of the Holocaust and today I cannot condone nor condemn their actions. However, having witnessed the attempted annilization of Judiasm in Europe, Irgun believed that the establishment of a free safe haven for Jewish people from around the world must be achieved at any cost.

How should we judge Irgun and Menachem Begin's past? When I think about him, the year 1978 comes to my mind. September of that year, he along with President Jimmy Carter and Anwar Sadat of Egypt signed the Camp David Accords. For one who was seen by many as a purveyor of terrorist ideology, his transformation in three short decades was also viewed by some as miraculous. In many ways I not only carry his name, Menachem, but also deep within me I hold the lessons he taught the world about conciliation, forgetting the past, and looking to the future."

Menachem was hired in early December of 1997 and immediately thrust himself into all aspects of the emerging project.

METAMORPHOSIS

Kuala Lumpur: 1997

During his lecture In the spring of 1995 Kevin O'Connell had outlined the planned Oregon State University/Israel Tilapia project. He also emphasized Oregon State's commitment to attracting more international students, with a target date for a new fulltime position in the summer of 1997.

For several days Ishmael thought about what O'Connell had said in his lecture. He began to sense that a door had been opened and a pathway for achieving his revenge against Israel might lie before him. He estimated he had two years until the position at OSU was established and the proposed tilapia project was submitted with the approval date for that project also in 1997.

Ishmael's life was now to have a singular objective, to devise a plan that would result in being hired by the International Students Office at Oregon State University. He realized, of course, that as Ishmael Abboud he had little chance of being selected for the position; however the individual named Terence Fitzroy would indeed be an excellent candidate. 'But

I'm not Fitzroy,' he mused. As he pondered the dilemma, the beginnings of an idea began to emerge. The plan would be high-risk and fraught with unforeseen obstacles. Any minute miscalculation could implode the entire scheme. Daunting as the task seemed, the answer was clear, he must apply for the position at Oregon State as Terence Fitzroy; in fact become Terence Fitzroy. Ishmael fixed himself a stiff scotch and silently called upon Allah. He sat quitely for severl hours in a darkened room ruminating for an answer. Then he experienced what surely was an answer. "Yes," he cried aloud, "with the help of the mighty one I can do this!"

Ishmael recognized that the critical key to the success of his plans was the remarkable physical and facial resemblance that he and Terry shared. But that fortunate fact was only a single obstacle to overcome. There were many other additional challenges that had to be resolved before he could present himself and his credentials as Terence Fitzroy in the application to Oregon State University.

One of the initial steps that Ishmael needed to implement was developing a close trusted relationship with Terry. To that end, he began to meet Terry regularly for drinks, dinners, the theater, and then critcally important, frequent sightseeing trips which provided an atmosphere of closeness and intimacy. Within several months it became apparent Terry literally adored Ishmael. Had Ishmael been willing the relationship would have likely become physically sexual. Ishmael carefully managed the relationship, explaining to Terry that he needed to "progress" slowly as their growing closeness was a totally new experience for him. Terry accepted Ishmael's explanation and in fact thanked him for his honesty.

A major step in his planning was convincing Terry to purchase a new home together which would signal an indication of Ishmael's longer term intentions. Terry was very pleased and they bought a modest bungalow in early 1996. Once established in their new home Ishmael began to focus on the matter of both having no living relatives or heirs. Surprisingly, on the first occasion he raised the matter, Terry agreed to the idea of pooling all of their financial resources into a single trust as an excellent idea, with the other being sole beneficiary of the assets. In establishing the trust and other financial instruments Ishmael carefully avoided photographs in the documents and had cleverly switched required fingerprints for access to accounts. The latter methodology was the brainchild of the mysterious contact who Ishmael would sometimes speak with on prepaid cell phones.

At this point in their relationship it become obvious Terry had completely accepted Ishmael not only as his mentor and trusted adviser, but additionally as his expected lover.

After they purchased the home and moved in together Ishmael spent hours gathering information from Terry about his life. He spent hours asking questions about his parents, his studies at Cambridge (including obtaining his academic transcripts) and his travels after graduation before coming to Indonesia. He spent considerable time quizzing Terry concerning all of his work related activities and social contacts in Kuala Lumpur.

Terry had a small bookstore that brought and sold rare and first edition books. Ishmael familiarized himself with all aspects of the business even assisting Terry on occasion, particularly with financial matters. Terry also accepted a limited number of private clients for tutoring in differing languages in which he was highly proficient. He was the sole employee of that business which he named "Languages and Linguistics."

By mid-July 1996 Ishmael had completed his planning and felt he had identified all of the steps necessary to reach his objectives.

That July their dentist, Dr. John Ho suddenly vanished. He never resurfaced and his body was never located. Later that month Ho's office was broken into during the night, although apparently nothing was missing. However, Ishmael's and Terry's dental records had mysteriously been switched.

In early December of that year a terrible tragedy struck their once quiet neighborhood. The police and fire officials determined a gas line had ruptured in Terry and Ishmael's house and a fearsome firestorm had reduced the home to ashes. In the rubble the official's discovered the charred remains of an individual. When Ishmael was interviewed by the police he identified himself as Terence Fitzroy. Based on further investigation, authorities confirmed that the body in the fire was a person named Ishmael Abboud. His identification was verified through dental records at the office of Dr. Ho's successor Dr. Bill Lee, who had never treated Terry or Ishmael after he assumed the practice. As he had done on previous occasions Ishmael purchased a prepaid cell phone, made a long distance call and then destroyed the phone.

Ishmael, now as Terry, succeeded the individual named Ishmael in the trust without question.

As the year 1996 quietly slipped into 1997, the individual named Terence Fitzroy contacted Oregon State University concerning the status of the proposed new position in their International Students Office. The contact confirmed that the position would be advertised later and he requested an application for the position, which he received shortly by e-mail. In addition to standard biographical information he noted three major required submissions for the application. 1) academic credentials; 2) work history and experience likely relevant for success in carrying out the responsibilities of the position; 3) and personal and professional references.

His academic records from Cambridge University would

meet the first requirement. The transcripts that Ishmael had requested included a photograph of Terry. The picture showed a long-haired, fully bearded young man some 20 years earlier, that was hardly recognizable as Terence appeared in 1996. Terry once told Ishmael that in his early years at Cambridge it was the "Bohemian" period of his life. Ishmael never really understood what he meant; possibly the unkempt nature of the picture was an indication.

To meet the requirements of work history and relevant experience, Ishmael demonstrated his high levels of creativity and also his resolve and resourcefulness. The information that he submitted with the application was mostly the fabrication of Ishmael's twisted but exceptional reservoir of intelligence. Oregon State University would be the recipient of a complete portfolio detailing the operations of a private school, Languages and Linguistics, owned and operated by an individual named Lawrence Gilmartin, who's primary teaching master was Terence Fitzroy. The information would include accolades for Fitzroy's exceptional teaching skills, work record, and commitment to each student he served.

Ishmael would later learn that particularly interesting and important to the Oregon State search committee was a series of personal journals (typed) and signed by Fitzroy, concerning his extensive travels after college throughout Asia, Europe, South America, and the Middle East. The committee especially noted the writers sensitivity to the differing cultures of the people he encountered.

Ishmael Abboud had indeed done his homework well.

Although Ishmael had spent countless hours in his quest to be hired at Oregon State University, he had not acted alone. He was able to enlist the expertise of contacts not only in Kuala Lumpur but also from the Middle East in forging of documents, signature replication and development of publications.

With the beginning of the new year, 1997, the frenetic pace of Ishmael's activities subsided and he relaxed and contemplated his next move. It occurred to him that a visit to Oregon State University would afford him the opportunity to see the campus, potentially gather information that could enhance his application for the position; also most importantly he might be able to meet individuals potentially serving on the interviewing committee. With his new passport (Terence Fitzroy), as all of his important documents had been destroyed in the fire, he arrived in Corvallis the second week of January.

In retrospect the visit was to be more fruitful that he could have imagined. In addition to exploring the entire campus, he had a number of extremely productive interactions with members of the international students staff; additionally he was able to meet several individuals who would serve on the recruitment team. On the return flight to Kuala Lumpur, nursing his third scotch, he felt almost euphoric. With his well -honed skills in evaluating individuals reactions to him, he felt assured that he had made a powerful and lasting positive impression on those he had met. Now on his next visit, the final lap in the race, he must finish first.

In April 1997 Oregon State University advertised for the fulltime position in their International Students Office. They received over one hundred applications for the position including a substantial number from outside of the United States. In two months the commmittee screened all of the applications and selected seven finalists. In July they unanimously hired a charismatic handsome fellow named Terence Fitzroy.

CHRISTMAS PARTY

Oregon State University: 1997

Terry thought. 'Not even six months on the job and here I am again at another of President Silva's "everyone is invited" affairs. A conglomeration of misfits from more than one morally bankrupt culture, in attendance. Only a few Muslims, however many Ahl al Kibab (people of the book), and also the mughfil (moronic and dumb) who don't know what to believe. Silva must like the Kaffirs of South Africa as well as the "wet backs" from Mexico as they are all over the place. There are chinks, cripples and a few who are like Ibn al Kalb (son of dog). Most are a cesspool of subhuman vermin; syncophants pandering to the arrogant leadership in this place.

'Oh Ishmael,' he suddenly thought, 'I must be cautious about thinking and using labels in Arabic, for I am now among them, the "Great Satans" of the West.'

Terry smiled. 'Ah yes, the president; Señor Dr. Manuel Ortega Soto Elias Silva and his wife. What kind of name is that? He doesn't realize that he is the butt of a campus joke as the first initial of his names put together spells Moses! I have heard it more than once; yes old Moses here to lead the children to the promised land.'

"Good evening President Silva."

"Let me see, you are, I'm sorry."

"Terry Fitzroy sir, from the International Students Office."

"Oh yes Terry, we met once briefly; my goodness you're looking especially handsome this evening."

"Why thank you Mr. President."

"No Terry, call me Manuel, this is not business, strictly fun and pleasure. You know Terry here at OSU we have a deep commitment to bring increasing numbers of international students to our campus. It is an institutional focus and priority, so you are a critical player in our desire to further diversify our student body and culture."

"Yes, Mr. President, I mean Manuel, it's a primary reason I was attracted to your institution."

"Oh goodness Terry I don't think you've met my wife Selena. Dear I'd like you to meet Terry Fitzroy who is one of our new staff members in our outreach efforts for international students."

For a moment Terry couldn't speak as before him stood a tall statuesque woman with large smoldering coal black eyes. It wasn't only her eyes that temporarily transfixed him; it was her jet black hair cascading gently around her shoulders and slender wrinkle-free neck. Her unblemished skin was the color of cinnamon/honey that seemed to glow in the brightly lit Christmas ornaments; her eyes gazed directly at him, radiating sensuality.

He composed himself and uttered a rather weak, "good evening it's a pleasure to meet you Selena."

She slowly extended her hand touching his upturned palm. A tingling sensation coursed up his arm into his chest and then downward to his torso and gently exploded into his groin.

"Selena, that's correct isn't it?"

"Yes Terry" she replied, his name seemingly tumbling over her large slightly parted lips, again causing another trembling within him.

The president remarked, "yes indeed, old Bosworth always seems to put together quite an affair; a lovely group here this evening. Well Selena and I need to move about, greet the troops, as they say, happy holidays Terry."

"Best wishes for special holiday season to both of you."

As he turned to leave the president glanced back at Terry and asked, "Terry are you okay, you look a bit dazed; did your encounter with Selena do that to you? She has a way of stopping fellows in their tracks the first time they meet her. Ha, ha!"

A faint angelic/wicked smile crossed Selena's face, her lustrous eyes shining as she demurely remarked, "Terry maybe later on we can have some time to chat a bit more; I look forward to learning more about you."

"Yes I'd like that," and he hurried off into the noisy group of holiday revelers.

'Almighty Allah was I that obvious ? I need to be more careful; maybe old Manuel isn't as slow as people say he is.'

As the president and Selena walked away it occurred to him that Manuel had said happy holidays, not Merry Christmas. 'What a phony; I know in the past he has made a big deal about being a devout Christian, a classic Catholic. Really? He's more of a cafeteria Catholic, a person who picks and chooses what he wants to believe that fits with his secular agenda. I have learned many people think the label is humorous; however the reality is that all those damnable Christians actually behave the same way. I'd wager he kisses the asses of all the Jewish folks here, wishing them a happy Hanukkah. That's not the way of Islam; true believers follow the Quran, the teachings of Muhammad without fail.'

As he left the president and Selena he pushed into the growing crowd of holiday revelers, fully shaken from her energy that had seemed to envelop him. He moved to the back of the ballroom, avoiding the crush of guests in an attempt to compose himself. He could see her across the floor.

"My god what a woman", he inadvertently whispered aloud.

"I beg your pardon,"asked a rather stuffy looking academic type who was walking by?

"Oh sorry, nothing just thinking out loud."

"Oh yes I see," replied the portly fellow, with a somewhat suspicious questioning reply. As he continued to gaze at Selena, his mind wandered to his youth and the first sighting of a desert gazelle; he recalled the eyes, almond shaped, bright, shining, transparent; windows into the soul of a free, wild, yet vulnerable, an exotic creation of mighty Allah.

'Oh no he thought, I have a vision of beauty in mind and who suddenly appears; old

Rory Spencer, that immoral homosexual, in our ancient writings, a Luti. I recently heard a guy label them as "canyon yodelers;" I thought that was pretty good. She is a big leader for women's rights. Women's rights, what kind of crap is that anyway? What Rory really needs is one night on the desert in the tent of a jumbo-sized Bedouin for an all night ride. She'd likely convert to Islam before sunrise.

Oh well, a curse on all of them. Where the hell is that guy Panzer?'

"There you two are, hello Kevin and Will."

"Hi Terry."

"I thought I would run into you two sooner or later; quite an affair isn't it?"

"Yes I guess you could say that everyone and his uncle is here; free food, free booze, and lots of bullshit. Will, you know if we could harvest all the crap flying around the room we would not have to buy any more for our greenhouse work!"

"Nah, that would not work, it's too full of viruses. It would kill all of the plants in a week. Ha!"

"Will have you met Terry from the International Students Office? He's one of our hot shot recruiters for international kids."

"No, we haven't met but I have heard about you, nice to meet you."

"Likewise, I've also heard good things about you Will and the work you and Kevin are doing."

"Terry, where are you from originally?"

"Well, I am not a purebred, I'm English and Indian."

"Indian, are you a dot or a feather?"

"I'm sorry, what do you mean dot or feather ?"

"Oh, I mean Indian from India or Indian from maybe the American West; like a Arapahoe or a Blackfoot. Say speaking of an Arapahoe and reminds me of a joke."

"Will, for Christ's sakes, why are you so damned intent on digging a hole for yourself the first time you meet someone?"

"Well it's a story of a simple question and I'm not making fun of anyone."

"Oh I see, no I'm not a feather type, I'm an Indian, from India."

"Nice to meet you Terry, you had me fooled, when you first walked up I had you pegged for a dude from the Middle East; I would have guessed Egyptian as you make me think of a good friend of mine from that area. I have been to Egypt numerouus times and I'm pretty good at spotting boys from the Nile."

Terry expperienced a moment of slight panic, but replied, "yes I understand."

He made a mental note to be cautious around Panzer in the future.

"Well, I know that some people think I might be Middle Eastern, an Arab or Jew because of my coloring. Actually my mother was from India and with my father from England, I came out not quite white and not quite a dark Indian."

There was an awkward pause, and Terry thought to himself, 'great Allah I need to get this guy on to another subject.'

"Hey Will I'm not easily offended I'd like to hear your joke if you don't mind."

"Great Terry, I could tell just looking that you are a guy who would like that story, so here goes.

These two black gals were riding on a train from Texas going West and entered the state of Arizona. Somewhere near Tucson two dark-skinned young ladies got on the train. One black lady said to the other, "sister look at those two, they really don't look black, and they really don't look white, what do you think they are?"

The other woman replied, "well let's ask them."

"Good idea."

They moved several seats back and sat down opposite the two new arrivals and said "we don't want to be rude, but we are curious about you two. You see we are black folks, but you two don't look black and you don't look white. What are you?"

One of the young women smiled and said, "oh you see, I'm a Navajo and my friend here is an Arapahoe, from up north."

"Well, what a small world said one lady from Texas, it's nice to meet you because my friend and I are a couple of Dallas 'hoes'."

Everyone exploded into laughter and the mood changed entirely. Kevin said, "I don't beelieve it Will; you seem about to fall into crap and come up smelling like a rose."

"Hey Kevin don't worry about it, that's a great joke. You

know when I came here in 1975 I wouldn't have had any idea about most of the American Indians. I didn't know any Arapahoe, Navajo, or for that matter one of those gals called an Ida-ho. See Kevin you're too uptight, relax, maybe we need to have another drink. Terry what do you like?"

"Well, being part English I'm partial to some of the great scotches; the stuff that we English borrowed from the Scots."

"Kevin let's test this dude and see what he really knows about scotch. Terry what is your favorite scotch?"

"I really like the single malts. For some reason I got hooked on anyone of the six classic Scots whiskys; Oban, Cragganmore, Talisher, Dalwhinnie, Lagavulan or Glenkinchie."

"Holy crap Kevin this guy is okay, anyone who knows enough to drink single malt scotch is a winner. Terry old boy you will be happy to know they have Cragganmore and also one of my favorites Glenmorangie. Come on let's get to the bar before some fool discovers they have single malt booze and drinks all of it. Ha!"

Already a bit "oiled" they pushed their way through the crowd to the bar and each one of them ordered a double. As promised, Will gladly picked up the tab as all the booze was free.

With none of them feeling any pain Terry recognized this might be a good time to inquire about the tilapia project with Israel. Both Will and Kevin were still feeling especially elated about the award. They would banter back and forth about the fact that they were on the cutting edge of the tilapia revolution. Predictably they were more than happy to share information about the project and proceeded to suggest they were about to become world leaders in tilapia growing and distribution. They lost sight of the fact that Terry had asked a question and continued to pontificate for the next several minutes. Their noisy enthusiasm was interrupted by an Egyptian professor from the College of Agriculture. His name was Hamdi and he had overheard the discussion of tilapia; particularly the implication that Americans had discovered their potential value. Hamdi wasn't shy himself and he interjected himself into the discussion with an opening remark, "Bullshit!. I need to inform you two hot shots that the Egyptians have known about tilapia for hundreds of years. We call them Boulti– Nile Tilapia. I know that you have a great project coming up with the Israelis and let me be the first to congratulate you. However, keep in mind we Egyptians knew about tilapia before there even was an America." He ended the scolding, abruptly turned and walked away. Then he stopped and remarked," sorry to interrupt, but I just had to straighten you guys out. See you later."

Terry breathed a sigh of relief as he privately was becoming a bit weary with all of the self-congratulary rhetoric. 'Thank goodness that fellow showed up, I was beginning to think about how I could get away without insulting them.'

As Hamdi walked away Will whispered, "what an ass hole; he's a typical arrogant Egyptian, who thinks he knows everything and trys to hang on to a past that is long gone.

Next time he interrupts I'm going to bring up the Six-Day War and see what he has to say about that."

Terry flinched noticeably and Kevin said, "hey man are you okay?"

"Oh no I'm fine, I guess I took too big to swallow of this classic scotch."

Will said, "hey I'm going to circulate a bit and try to get some gossip on who's screwing who these days."

Terry replied, "good idea, I'm going to see if there's any good looking women hiding out."

The three of them went their separate ways and Terry found his way outside to the balcony overlooking the campus. He was visibly shaken by the interaction of both Will and Hamdi. He leaned over the railing and thought to himself, 'in the name of Allah I must get control of myself. These two guys have strong egos, are very sure of themselves and don't mind letting others know what they think. Those are great qualities, but we have very different agendas and I have to be extremely cautious. Both Will and Kevin are really quick on the uptake and I could see a single spoken word might set off an alarm in their extremely well –wired grey matter.'

Sometime later Terry got himself another drink and thought about the previous incident. Suddenly he had a flash of clarity in his thinking. I know what I need to do; I can't run away from those two, I need to work closely with them as they are likely very important to my future plans. They love their project and need to talk about it; publicity, that's what they want and that is what I can give them. I need to find them and float the idea. Maybe with a few more single malts they might get magnanimous and I could have a new job.

He found the two "Tilapia Cowboys" as they liked to call themselves these days. He ordered another round of drinks and carefully outlined his ideas for a major publicity campaign for the project with himself guiding the process. Within ten minutes, in rather uproarious fashion, they declared the idea was great and they would speak to the president, if not tonight, within the next couple of days and get him transferred to the project. Surprised, Ishmael murmured to himself, "praise be to Allah, that was easier than I thought it would be."

Will said, "speaking of the president, what do you guys think of his wife; is she a knockout or what?"

"Yes she is, replied Kevin, but I understand she is from Oaxaca which puzzles me."

"Why do you say that, asked Will?"

"Well the people from Oaxaca are often quite small, that is short; many of the people are Zapotec Indians, and they are little guys. Also she's very fair skined, more like a Castilian Spaniard."

Will replied, "well I'd guess there was probably a honkie in the family tree somewhere along the line. You know with Maximilian running the show for awhile in Mexico there surely was a good number of European types immigrating to the country."

Ishmael nodded and thought 'yes that likely could be the case.'

He began to wander through the crowd looking for the president and his wife, especially for the wife.

He soon found her again, seated in a somewhat secluded alcove. He thought, 'she is like a queen holding court.' Guests aimlessly strolling by would recognize her and stop to chat. She was eloquent, graceful, welcoming each person, gently touching them, flashing a brilliant smile for some, others a coquettish sensual parting of her lips. She saw Terry and motioned him to come to her.

'I must make the most of this opportunity he thought;' he felt that his strong attraction to her was not only noticed by Selena, but he felt that she had also experienced some similar feelings in meeting him.

They chatted briefly about inane topics for a few minutes and then surprisingly she said, "I understand you work in student services recruiting international students. Is that right?"

"Why yes, I love my position, but also hope to become more involved in the new tilapia project."

"Terry," she almost purred, "I'd like to hear more about what you do to recruit international students; would you be willing to have lunch and quench the curiosity of an older woman?"

Again, Terry was almost floored. He took a deep breath, and

to his surprise was only able to faintly reply, "why of course, I would be more than happy to fill you in."

They arranged to have lunch the first week in January.

LE RENDEZVOUS

January: 1998

El Cisne (the Swan) was an upscale dining restaurant in downtown Corvallis; somewhat of an oddity for semi- rural Oregon as it was known for serving excellent cuisine native to the Mexican state of Oaxaca.

It was the primary reason that Selena had suggested to Terry they meet there for lunch the first week of January 1998.

She was already seated when he arrived. Once again, as when they met initially at the Christmas party, he found himself somewhat flustered. It was Selena's appearance and demeanor that seemed to temporarily numb his ability to respond. She was dressed, more accurately adorned, in a brilliant red and blue suit, which accented her slim well proportioned figure. Lustrous black hair cascaded down her shoulders and her perfectly formed lips carried a red sheen; it was her smoky black eyes, fixed intently on him, carrying a subtle almost evil sensuality, which caused him to be unsettled.

"You see Terry, isn't this a lovely setting? What a wonderful view of the river front, don't you agree?"

Rather weakly he replted, "Yes, very nice; I take it you must have been here before?"

"Oh yes of course, she smiled, many times; it is one of my favorites. The menu is extensive and really wonderful."

"I see or assume it has a strong Latin American flavor."

"Oh Terry, much more than that; it features entrees from the place of my youth and heritage, Oaxaca."

"Yes, I recall Kevin or Will at the Christmas party mentioning that you had come from Oaxaca."

"Yes my great-grandfather went (rather was deported) from Sonora to Oaxaca, in 1903 by Porfirio Diaz."

"Why was that?"

"Great granddad an engineer from Germany, had gone to Mexico around 1890 to string telegraph lines for the government. After five years or so he got lonely and married a young Yaqui girl. At the time there was much conflict between the government and the Yaqui's."

"Why the conflict?"

"Well, I'm not totally sure but I do know that Yaquis were fiercely independent, warriors or raiders, depending on which side you choose to believe. Our family folklore says that his wife Maria Perez was a daughter of Cajeme (Jose Maria Bonifacio Leyba Perez), a militant Yaqui warrior. After a highly successful military career fighting the French (for Mexico) Cajeme was rewarded with an appointment that was essentially the mayor of the the Yaquis. Expected to pacify them, instead he united the people and demanded self-government. As Mexico would not tolerate self-government, a series of brutal conflicts ensued leading to Cajeme's capture and execution in 1887. I'm sorry to bother you with all this family history, but you see I'm a fiercely proud descendant of that gallant warrior."

"Oh no, Mrs. President."

"Stop right there Terry, I'm Selena to you – okay?"

"Yes of course Selena, and what a wonderful heritage you have. I love history and I am going to dig into this fellows background, Cajeme, is that the name?"

"Yes he was an exceptional man."

"Truly, that is a great story."

"I heard that the tilapia cowboys were discussing my heritage, wondering why I am so tall and fair skinned. Silly boys, I'm not a Zapotec, I'm Yaqui and German. Ha!

Hey, Selena blurted out let's eat, I'm starving and they have a great menu. For starters we could have a bean/guacamole tostado which is especially good with a Cadillac margarita. Then two of my favorite entrees are Mole Negro De Pollo- Oaxacan, chicken with Dark Mole or Cecina Adobada, marinated pork with twenty+ spices."

"Sounds wonderful, you order Selena."

"Good, another time I'll tell you the story of our family's move from Oaxaca to Mexico City when I was ten years old.

Terry do you want to try the specialties of the house, and if so, chicken or pork?"

"I'll have the chicken with chocolate sauce."

"No no Terry, it's called Mole, and I think you will enjoy it."

The Cadillac margaritas arrived as they waited for the meal. Service was elegant which allowed time for a second margarita. Their meal arrived and Terry remarked, "my goodness Selena these margaritas are indeed Cadillac; I'm feeling a bit numb and mellow."

Selena flashed a sensuous smile, leaned forward and whispered seductively, "well that's good, the nectar of the agave not only will carry away your troubles, but can also loosen one's inhibitions and open the paths to new and unimagined delights; don't you agree?"

Terry didn't respond, rather looked into her eyes, sensing that this elegant lady had just opened a door and issued an invitation. He lowered his head, then looked back at her, smiled, and said "Selena, you are a very alluring and provocative woman, do you realize that?" With a faint giggle she replied, "yes, dear Terry, other men have said the same of me; I don't mind especially if that man does find me, what did you say, alluring; and do you?"

"I think you know my answer as I belive you guessed my thoughts that night we first met at the Christmas party. Selena let's eat before I whisk you away and manhandle you like a Bedouin on his wedding night."

"Terry, what a strange comment, Bedouin I mean; maybe you are really a bad fellow." Terry, startled by her comment, paused for an instant but quickly recovered; he replied "on the contrary Selena many have said I am quite good."

The sexual fencing ended and they enjoyed the exceptional cuisine of El Cisne and a fine red wine. They ordered coffee and Selena said "okay Terry, my turn, tell me about yourself – Indian and English you say? That sometimes obstreperous guy Panzer thought maybe you were an Arab. Ha! Are you?"

Again Terry experienced a visceral jerk in his stomach, thinking 'does this wench have suspicions of me'? He recouped his middle eastern bravado and replied, "why of course my lady, in prep school I was sometimes known as the son of the Sheik of Araby."

"Seriously Terry why did they call you the Sheik?"

"Oh, I think it was because of my dark dashing good looks and powerful physique and other masculine attributes."

"My goodness Terry, once again I'm not sure what to think of your remarks; do I need to be on guard around you?"

Terry laughingly remarked, "who can tell Selena, maybe the future will soon provide an answer."

With a slight tilt of her head and a soft lilting chuckle she said "yes I agree, I think we shall soon see; now back to who is one Terry Fitzroy?"

"Would you like the long or abbreviated version of my Life?"

"The limited version is fine for now as these spirits have me a bit foggy."

"Fine, but don't leave out any exciting or mischievous deeds."

"Okay, listen carefully."

Ishmael paused for a moment collecting his thoughts silently reminding himself that he was relating the lineage of Terry Fitzroy, not himself. He had spent hours memorizing details of Terry's past and now he must carefully reconstruct what he knew.

"I was born in London in 1955 at my parents townhouse. I was the only child of Malcolm Fitzroy and his Indian Princess Karishma."

"Terry what were the circumstances that led to your father marrying a woman from India?"

"Let me back up a bit on family history. My grandfather Hugh Fitzroy owned a tea plantation in Darjeeling West Bengal India. He went to India when he was twelve years old as his father worked in the tea export business. Old Hugh was an entrepreneurial old devil and started buying or stealing land from the Indians. At age twenty-six he had his own tea plantation."

"Terry, you mean to tell me that your grandfather was a thief stealing land from those poor Indians?"

"Well, that's only family folklore I really don't know."

"Sounds familiar to me, that is what the Mexicans did to my Yaqui ancestors."

"Hugh's wife, again I don't know much about her, died in childbirth when my father Malcolm was born in 1920. Father inherited the plantation in 1950 when Hugh died."

"Terry that's about enough family history, let's get to the Princess."

"Yes, I'm almost there. My father married the daughter of an Indian Raj, Nilmoni Singha Dev. He and his wife Churmoni had one daughter and named her Karishma (which means miracle). I don't know why they called her that name, maybe the childbirth was difficult. She was Hindu but my father never went to church, so religion, the hereafter, etc. was not a part of my life or upbringing."

"What about you growing up?"

"I had a nanny, a kind elderly lady that I knew as Ms. Prudence."

"Where did you live?"

"Ha, mostly in boarding schools; Caldicott prep school seven – thirteen years old in the village of Farnham in Buckingham Shire; then on to Harrow who's alumni include Church-Hill, Nehru, and King Hussein – aren't you impressed ? Then on to Cambridge."

"Terry that's enough, tell me the rest of your life at our next lunch. Let's have another round before we go."

"Are you sure? I can really feel those Cadillacs and the wine."

"Come on Terry just a small digestif; we can share a Sambuca and coffee, anise flavored."

"Good."

They sipped the sweet- flavored coffee and chatted idly. They left and Terry walked her to her car. She unlocked the door and turned to Terry, her eyes sparkling, her full lips parted. "Did you enjoy lunch Terry?"

"Why yes very much."

"So did I and let's meet again soon for another rendezvous."

"Rendezvous you say, is that what our lunch was?"

"Yes, that's what it was for me,"she replied.

She reached out, embraced Terry tightly and then grasped his face with both hands and kissed him passionately.

"Does that tell you how much I enjoyed our brief time together today?"

"Yes, it surely does Selena; I look forward to our next encounter."

VISIT TO THE GAN

January: 1998

January in Oregon can be a miserable time -it rains, and the next day it rains again, but the next several days it doesn't rain, it pours!

It was the middle of January when Terry and Will were having a freshly brewed cup of "Seattle's finest." Suddenly Will blurted out, "Jesus Christ Terry why are we sitting here getting our butts soaked everyday when we could be on a plane to the land of milk and honey?"

"What what do you mean," asked Terry?

"Well, I think it's about time that we take a fact-finding or maybe a fact- sharing trip with the president to Israel for an update on the project. You know the boys start thinking about budgets around this time of year and it surely wouldn't hurt to show old Manuel what a couple of studs he has working for him, like you and me. Yes, time to start jacking up those salaries. Ha!"

"Will, sometimes you really surprise me; that's really a great idea."

"Hey do you think we can take that sexy broad, his wife, along? We don't want the President to get lonesome over there. I'm not sure how friendly those Israeli ladies would be to Manuel; who knows they might think he's an Arab or even worse a Palestinian."

"Well, maybe we shouldn't take him along, hell, some crazy old Israeli might try to whack him."

"Yes, that would probably not be too good for the project; it would really piss off Kevin and furthermore with the president dead it could blow our raises."

"Ha, ha!"

"No actually, I think the trip is a good idea Will. Let's get together with Kevin and develop a strategy outlining objectives, an itinerary, and timetable; a couple of weeks over there should be about right."

"Sure, he has to see all the highlights of the place, especially Jerusalem, the Wailing Wall, the Dome of the Rock, Golgatha, and whatever."

"Say how about a good Jewish cat house?"

"No, no, you forget Mrs. is going to be along, so none of that guys only stuff."

"OK, you're right."

"Let me call Kevin to set a time to meet and see what he thinks."

Kevin was in fact ready to get a on a plane the day they met. It was Tuesday, and when Terry called and explained what he and Will had discussed, he cleared his morning calendar and met with them at 9:00 AM.

"Well, we're around four months into the project and old Menachem is really making great progress; he's very sharp and a hard working motivator. Since he isn't in the military any longer if you don't follow orders he can't court martial you, he just kicks the crap out of you."

They all laughed and Will speculated, "you know from what I have read, he reminds me of old George Patton; boy would those two have been a pair. Those "Russkies" wouldn't have gotten within one hundred miles of Berlin."

"You know, Kevin, where have we gone astray as people? What happened to the good old days when you shot first and asked questions later?"

"Holy smokes Will that's a bit rough"

"What do you mean a bit rough? Look at the history of our country just one hundred years ago. You didn't have a bunch of politically correct "do- gooders" telling you what to say and how to behave. This country, particularly the West was raw and wild; to survive one had to be decisive and know who your friends and enemies were; then you behaved accordingly."

"Sure, people had to take responsibility for their own survival, that didn't necessarily translate into open warfare with any one who looked cross-eyed at you."

"I'm not saying that; what if you got caught out on the plains by a mean spirited Blackfoot who intended to take a hunk of your head off? Would you first try conciliation? Like, now can't we all just be friends or if you must lift my hair, could you just take a little off the top? No, if you wanted to wake up the next day you would have to shoot the guy on the spot even if it did violate his civil rights."

"Will, what the devil has gotten into you this morning? Does thinking about going to Israel make you put on a blood thirsty mantle to dispose of anyone you suspect is a terrorist?"

Kevin interupted, "hey, hey stop all the bull crap, let's get back to the agenda. Terry would you call the president's office and see if he can schedule a meeting for later this week. Tell him if it's just to give him an idea of what we have in mind; we can work out the details later."

Lynda, the president's executive assistant answered the telephone.

"Good morning President Silva's office, how may I help you?"

"Gee Lynda, have you been demoted? I thought only the underlings answered the phone up there in the ivory tower."

"This Is Terry isn't it?"

"Yes, how did you know?"

"Oh, I can recognize your voice. You know Terry you keep in touch with our office on a regular basis. If I didn't know better I might think you had some dark nefarious scheme up your sleeve."

"Well, as a matter of fact my pretty lady I do. Lynda it's OK if I refer it to you as pretty lady isn't it?"

"Not really, but you will anyway. Don't worry I just let your sugar coated baloney fly over my head. What can I do for you today?"

"Seriously Lynda, Kevin O'Connell, Will Panzer, and I would like to meet with the president as soon as possible, hopefully this week. We think the timing is such that the president ought to be looking in on the tilapia project in Israel. I'm sure he would like to get out of this lousy weather for a few days. Does he have a spot on his calendar this week were you could fit us in?"

"Gosh Terry this week is really busy and he has a full schedule; I don't know."

"Well see what you can do; maybe we only need thirty to forty-five minutes to test the waters to see if he's interested."

"OK Terry give me an hour and I'll talk to him. Here is my cell phone number call me back."

Terry called Lynda back in exactly one hour and she had set the meeting for two days later at 10:00 AM. He arrived early for the meeting, which was deliberate, as he had learned that arriving early or unannounced often paid dividends. Lynda was in the outer office and she remarked, "why Terry you're early this morning."

"Oh I guess I am, I wasn't paying attention to the time."

"Really?" She gave him a smirk, a bit of a wink and retreated into her private office. Ishmael thought to himself, 'I need to be careful around this woman-she could be dangerous; she has an extremely sharp mind.' He watched her leave, sort of glide away, more of a sensuous stroll. She was physically very attractive, highly intelligent, and her ability to fend off attempted masculine flattery, only heightened her captivating demeanor. Lost in thought, he began to fantasize sexually about her; more importantly to reprimand himself to be more cautious in future encounters with her." Allah be praised for the creation of such exotic creatures, he murmured to himself." Kevin and Will arrived and glanced at Terry. Will chriped, "Terry what's up, you look awful; you look like someone dragged you through a knot hole. Are you OK?"

"Yes, I'm fine, I guess I was thinking about the meeting with the president and didn't hear you come in."

They were ushered into the president's office and Manuel greeted them with a cheerful, "Good morning gentlemen." He smiled broadly and and continued with "I'm not sure if I think of you characters as the three musketeers or the three amigos!"

"How's that sir," Terry asked?

"Well it seems to me anytime your names are linked together I can expect the unexpected."

Terry smiled and said, "you know sir if you have any suspicions you might want to focus on those Israelis, instead of us. They are really a crafty bunch of guys and have now appointed two people to the international advisory committee for the project. You know about Landau, but now they've added a director of public relations. I don't know any details

Mr. President, but my information is that an inner circle of men made the decision without any input."

"How's that?"

"Well, the individual hired was a former Miss Israel, Noya Siegel. I hear that she is really gorgeous, maybe not the sharpest knife in the drawer, but they believe she can handle the position."

"Yes I understand, to be honest I was aware of the appointment, but as an ex-officio member of the advisory committee I hereby declare my innocence in the hire. Ha! That matter is more like something that you three guys would pull off."

"Sir, you surely know that our behaviors are only focused on the best interests of the university and the project."

"Why of course I do!"

They briefly outlined the idea of the trip to Israel and Manuel responded quickly, "as a matter of fact I agree that a trip to see the operation first hand is a good idea. I'll have Lynda begin making arrangements and calling people to see if they would be available."

Kevin said, "as you know Will and I have been to Israel almost monthly, monitoring the program, but having you and Terry along this time would be important."

"Of course, I think it would be a good idea to have a nice contingent to meet with the project personnel. It would seem to me to signal our continuing commitment to the program."

Terry asked, "when do you think you can get away sir?"

"Gentlemen, please pardon my French, but with this shitty weather I'm ready to go anytime. Barring any major commitments I suggest we try to get away within the next two weeks. I'll have Lynda contact Menachem and see if that would be good for them. Oh, I want to contact Senator Wyden and Earl Blumenauer to see if they can get away; they probably can, especially since I'll agree to fund the trip.!"

The president asked, "do you feel a week stay is enough time to get a good look at the project, meet the right people and have a little time to see some of the country? Gosh, maybe we'd even have time to get to Jerusalem?"

"Kevin replied, I believe we could pretty much get a good sense of how the project is going in a week. I think we could likely see the physical plant in a day or two. Meetings with staff, both senior and worker types, shouldn't take at most two days. It would also be good to spend time(maybe two days) discussing preliminary issues such as celebrations, dedication, publicity, invitees etc. at completion of the project. What's your take Will?"

"Yes I agree, maybe a week on Gan matters and another two or three days for some sightseeing."

"OK, I hear you guys, maybe ten days would be better. I'll have Lynda schedule a time for both of you to give me a full report on the project." They were able to meet three days later and provide a comprehensive briefing on progress to date.

VISIT TO The GAN - A COUP

January: 1998

Terry, Will and Kevin met for coffee the morning after their briefing with the president concerning
the progress of the Gan project.

"Kevin asked, how do you feel the meeting yesterday with President Silva came off?"

Will responded, "I think it went very well and Old Manny has what he needs, as long as he doesn't get distracted by Miss Israel."

Terry was silent, seemingly in thought.

"Terry, no comment, you look puzzled?"

"No, I was thinking about that guy Landau who has already been appointed to the advisory committee. I understand, he will also have some ongoing involvement with the project. He's a lawyer and an accomplished musician; violin I think. On top of that he's handicapped from polio, contracted as a child."

Will jumped in and barked, "boy those crafty Israelis aren't wasting any time loading the project with their people. First Miss Israel, now Landau and let's not forget the project director Allon. Well at least we got the guy we wanted, Dr. Don Lightner from the University of Arizona."

"From where?" Asked terry.

"The Environmental Research Lab, theUniversity of Arizona; there isn't anything he doesn't know about shrimp and fish pathogens. He's literally number one in the world."

Terry smiled, "why don't we see if we can get Silva to also appoint someone to the committee like Netanyahu did."

Before Terry could continue, Will interrupted excitedly and exclaimed, "wow I have the perfect person in mind, Ray Charles!"

"You mean the singer Ray Charles?"

"Yes, if Netanyahu can put a handicapped dude on the committee we'll retaliate, and steal his thunder with our own gimp."

"Gimp, what kind of slur is that Will?"

"Gimp, that's not a slur, when I was at the University of Illinois that was how the handicapped kids refered to themselves. You were either a gimp or an AB, able- bodied person."

"Holy smokes Will, that still sounds bad."

"Relax Kevin, besides Ray Charles would be honored. We'd have him sing, Georgia On My Mind at the opening ceremony next spring. The people would love him. Say even better, we could have that guy Landau accompany him on the violin."

"Will, where in hell do you come up with these hair -brained asinine ideas? Are you really serious?"

"Absolutely, I think he would really be a positive addition; you know his version of Georgia is now the state song of Georgia. We would make sure that everyone at the opening ceremony was aware of that great honor. What do you think?"

Terry jumped in. "Well, it might be OK, Silva might like it; especially with his focus on having every variety of human being on the planet included in the mix. Let's talk to him."

Kevin paused, thought for a moment and responded, "well maybe it is an idea worth pursuing, but let me talk to the president about the idea, not you two. I don't think there's any rush to get a decision."

"Will said, I have it; maybe we should spring the idea on him and the Israelis later on, like a trump card, just before the opening."

Kevin groaned and shook his head.

That ended the discussion and Will left chuckling to himself as he knew the idea where surely going to be a great coup.

VISIT TO THE GAN- DELAYED

January: 1998

Netanyahu's aide Benjamin Edelman remarked, "the Americans seem to be a bit pesky don't you think? None of us understand why the sudden urgency to visit the project construction site. There is really nothing much to see other then unfinished greenhouses, buildings and a huge array of equipment and people running all over the place like a bunch of ants."

Menachem Allon, the project site director was a bit harsher in his comments. "You know in the past months after meeting some of their people, namely those guys Panzer and O'Connell, I get the distinct impression they think they're doing Israel a huge favor allowing us to locate the project here in the Arava Valley. The location of the project was primarily an Israeli idea; someone ought to remind them of that fact."

Edelman interjected, "OK Menachem, maybe you see it that way, but a primary issue is Netanyahu couldn't get away and furthermore he felt a visit now would only be disruptive for the ongoing work."

Eli Efron, the the construction superintendent echoed the sentiment. "We have enough problems daily trying to stay on schedule; can you imagine a large contingent of gawkers asking hundreds of inane questions for several days maybe even longer. I believe I heard they were planning to bring ten or eleven people."

David Landau had listened quietly but then added. "There Is another Issue that many won't consider even at this early stage of the game; that is the matter of security. We really aren't in a position to do a thorough background check on everyone who would be coming."

"Oh for goodness sakes David why are you so superstitious of everyone and everything? I Sometimes wonder if you are suffering from paranoia?"

"Wait a minute, wait a minute Noya. What do we know about the people who would be coming to visit the site. We do know the president of their university, the two men who were the major developers of the grant, O'Connell and Panzer, but who is the other guy Fitzroy? He's in the international students office, hired from Southeast Asia, running a bookstore or something in Kuala Lumpur. What's his background?"

Noya jumped in once again. "David we all know your history and the two instances in which essentially your instincts and abilities of observation literally saved dozens of lives; all of Israel thanks you for that. How you were able to spot those murderous terrorists was indeed remarkable. Some believe you have an almost supernatural ability to observe, decipher and project behavior. My mother once remarked, Yahweh took your legs but in return gave you a brilliant mind."

Levi interrupted, "hey I know David has a great mind, but I think I know the real story, he's a buddy of Menachem Begin."

Noya asked, "what are you talking about?"

"Well we all know that Begin loved David's music, who

doesn't? I'm guessing that for a few private concerts old PM Begin likely taught him all the tricks he utilized to hunt down the Brits. and Arabs when he was in the Irgun. David are you Begin's secret agent? Ha!"

Everyone erupted with laughter, except David who winched, feeling the blood drain from his face.

"Hold on shouted Ben above the "hilarity." The task here today is to draft a response to the Americans, specifically to President Silva that outlines why now is just not a good time to entertain visitors to this site. Let's get down to listing the difficulties."

David breathed a silent sigh of relief. He thought, 'that blasted Allon, thankfully no one followed up on what they thought was an absurd question. I'm sure he doesn't know how close to the truth was his query. His instincts must come from the genes of his father.'

Once Edelman restored order he addressed the members of the meeting. "Here's how I think we can proceed; that is of course if all of you agree. Would each of you do a brief recap of the discussion today, listing reasons why the timing isn't good now for a visit from the Americans. Once I get all of your input I'll do a draft and send each of you a copy for any changes or corrections. Then I'll get a final version, and if OK, send it off to President Silva."

Noya asked, "what about Netanyahu? Don't you think he will want a final look at it?"

"Noya I have already asked him that question and I'll tell you what he said, and I quote, hell no!"

They adjourned, Benjamin drafted the letter, and after changes and additions were made, it was sent off to President Silva.

A week after the meeting with President Silva (concerning the visit to the tilapia project), Will and Kevin were having morning coffee in the student union when Terry walked in.

"Hey Terry what's up?" Will asked. "You look like you got your Johnson caught in your zipper."

That prompted a good laugh from Kevin, but Terry only grimaced, shook his head and remarked, "well Will if you think you're clever, I'd like to hear your response to my little bit of news."

"Fire way," retorted Will, "we're having a good start to the day and nothing can throw water on our parade."

"Oh really; well take this news flash and let's see what wise comment you have for this one."

"OK, OK let's hear it."

"The trip to Israel is off. The Jews don't want us to come right now."

"What are you saying? We're not going? What's the problem? Who told you this?"

Kevin jumped in; "hold on Will, for christ's sake slowdown, instead of a barrage of questions let's hear What Terry has to say."

"Thanks Kevin. Lynda called me just thirty minutes ago and said Manuel received a fax from Israel explaining why they really don't think this is a good time to visit."

"Why not? What difference does it make when we go?"

"Damn it Will shut up and and let Terry finish."

"OK, OK."

"The fax the president received listed a number of reasons why the Israelis feel a visit now would not only be counterproductive but also could be disruptive and and cause delays in ongoing construction initiatives. Even the matter of security was apparently raised by that guy Landau."

"Security, what security? Do those paranoid Israelis think were coming to sabotage the project? Somebody needs to remind them that were on the same team."

"I Know Will, but Landau stated they were not in a position to do background checks on a large contingent of people."

"That's ridiculous! Do they think we have a secret agent in our group who is committed to the destruction of Israel? Oh I get it, Landau suspects that Manuel Silva isn't really Mexican, rather an Arab and likely a terrorist."

"Will, wait a minute."

"No let me finish. Maybe they suspect Manuel is going to smuggle a bomb into the facility and at some point the bomb will go off and blow the place to kingdom come."

"C'mon Will, that's enough knock it off!"

"No, I'm almost finished. The blast will annihilate everyone nearby, but of course old Manuel will miraculously survive."

Terry shuttered, held his breath and thought to himself, 'that damn Will, he goes off trying to be funny; what if someone takes his rantings seriously?'

Kevin remarked, "look, it's apparent they have concerns and I can understand that a large group arriving now could be disruptive, interfere with the work schedules and really accomplish very little."

"Oh I know," smirked Will, "I'm joking; you know me, a little levity on bad news is like ice cream on a few tirds- makes it more palatable."

Everyone laughed including Terry. Apparently neither Will or Kevin had noticed Terry's discomfort with Will's outburst.

"Lynda said the president has already responded with an OK on delaying the trip; he also commited to staying in touch with the project director to set a firm date for a visit. A tentative timeline for later this year would likely be October or November. I'll get back to Lynda and let her know that you have been informed. However, you can be sure I'm not going to share any of the outrageous speculations I heard, especially about President Silva."

Kevin and Will again laughed appreciatively and asked Terry, "would you like to join us for quick cup?"

"No thanks, I have to get back to work; that's what I do."

On the way back to his office Terry was still a bit shaken by Will's antics. He thought, 'that Panzer likes to play the fool. Maybe it's for the attention he gets, but I think he's dangerous. He may need to be dealt with in the future.'

MANUEL AND SELENA SILVA - ROOTS

March: 1998

"Aha, Cadillac margaritas! That's why El Cisne is your favorite place to eat, isn't it? I understand the Oaxaca connection, your heritage and the food, but it's the elixir of the agave, right?"

Selena giggled, "oh Terry I suppose it's a little of both."

"Well I vividly recall my last encounter with your favorite tequila and what I remember most is being in a fog."

They both laughed as they were seated for dinner. Manuel was out of town and they decided on a late evening dinner. Since their first luncheon engagement in early January they had met on several occasions. During their second meeting any pretense concerning the nature of their relationship vanished in an extended orgy of sexual passion. They both agreed that these trysts had to remain completely discreet. Selena made it clear that she would never leave Manuel under any circumstances. Furthermore, she was candid telling him that a primary reason for not leaving Manuel was the luxurious lifestyle that his wealth provided her. Likewise Terry confessed to Selena that his position at Oregon State was a "dream job" and he would do nothing that might jeopardize his employment at the university. The sexual relationship with Selena was highly gratifying and enjoyable, but his commitment to ensuring unwavering discretion was essentially camouflaging a more sinister objective for Terry.

On the occasion that Selena told Terry that she would remain loyal to Manuel, as money was a major reason, he asked Selena how Manuel had acquired all of his wealth.

"Selena, Manuel appears to be to be so easygoing, I just don't imagine him as an individual who would aggressively pursue making money."

"No, no, the family fortune was accumulated in a relatively short span of years by Manuel's father, Renaldo Silva, who possesed an outstanding legal mind. However, a second characteristic that fueled his meterotic rise was his total disdain for the ethics of his profession. In 1944, at the age of twenty-eight, Renaldo, who had been a fervent supporter of Manuel Camacho (elected president of Mexico in 1940), joined the Camacho administration as a legal adviser in the president's office. In only two years he established a brilliant reputation helping guide political policies and decisions that resulted in enormous and unprecedented profitability not only for the president, but also notably for Renaldo Silva.

His legal skills and financial savy were so highly valued that his career continued in essentially the same capacity as a legal adviser to presidents in the ensuing five administrations; culminating with his retirement at the age of sixty from the the Echeverria presidency in 1976.

In his position as legal adviser he was privy to information that enabled him to invest, buy and sell land, commodities and investments which often lead to enormous profits.

Renaldo was not only shrewd and aggressive but he was also

a born gambler. His entire career was not unlike an unending poker game; he seldom lost a wager, as he almost always knew the outcome for each hand when the cards were dealt.

Manuel, very unlike his father, (mostly absent during Manuel's early years) had little interest in learning about making money. He was not interested in corporate warfare, rather, he embodied the more gentle, sensitive, cautious qualities and values of his mother."

They finished dinner and left for Terry's. When they arrived Terry remarked, "Selena take a look around this place as we won't be coming here anymore."

Startled, Selena asked, "Terry, what do you mean? Is this a sudden brush off? "

"No, no not a chance for you to dump me. I've decided I'm going to move to Eugene."

"Why Terry?"

"Well, a number of reasons. First of all I'm really more of a private type person then maybe I appear. I honestly don't like being surrounded by the university crowd that seems to be everywhere one turns."

"Terry have you forgotten that Eugene has a little school called the University of Oregon? What will be different?"

"True, but I don't work at the University of Oregon, so most people I meet in town won't have any idea who I am or what I do. Honestly I have enough contact with my colleagues at Oregon State and I do like getting away from all the pandering."

They were sitting on the sofa and Terry moved closer to Selena and placed one hand on her thigh. He looked at her intently, lowered his voice, and slowed his rate of speaking. "More importantly Selena I get a bit nervous about us, that is, I'd much rather have you come to my abode in Eugene for frolic and lust. I just think there is much less chance of some fool blundering into the middle of a full blown marathon of sexual depravity."

"C'mon Terry, depravity ?"

"Selena just think about it; in Eugene we will have our own secluded sexual sanctuary."

His change in demeanor had the intended effect on Selena. Suddenly blushing and breathing heavily, she abruptly took his head in her hands and kissed him violently. They both began undressing themselves and each other, almost ripping their clothes off, leaving them in a trail to the bedroom. Their love-making was frenzied and noisy, entangled in the throes of sexual urgency. They showered together and Selena coyly but admiringly remarked "I know you have a name for that marvelous male sword you display, does it have a name?"

"Yes Selena it does; his name is Caesar, but we're not here to praise him, rather I am here to bury him."

Selena laughed. "Oh yes, I know what you mean, and I concur."

Later relaxing with a scotch, Terry asked, "Selena, at our first luncheon you said you would tell me more about your youth, growing up, and also about Manuel; how you two met."

"Terry do you want the condensed version or all of the excruciating details?"

"Selena I do enjoy history and particularly people's roots; how about the latter?"

"OK my dear, you asked for it. My great grandfather Herman Hofmeister was an engineer."

"Are you serious, Herman Hofmeister?"

"Terry don't interrupt me, you want all the details, so here they are."

"Back to old Herman. He was born in 1865 in northern Germany and went to Mexico in 1893 to install telegraph lines. He got lonely and in 1895 married a young Yaqui girl named Maria Perez. In 1897 they had a son and obviously compromised on his name, calling him Jose Wilhelm Perez."

"You're joking, they really tossed in Wilhelm, that's hilarious!"

"Terry stop it or I won't tell you anything more."

"OK, OK."

"Wait a minute, you say his name was Jose Perez, not Jose Hofmeister?"

"Yes that's right. I don't know the story, but the name Hofmeister was dropped for the surname Perez. Maybe it was just a simple matter that Hofmeister was too difficult to pronounce; who knows."

"I already told you about the conflict in Sonora between the government and Yaquis. Porfiro Diaz, EL Presidente, deported many Yaquis to Oaxaca in 1903."

"Now anything more about that man you mentioned Cajeme?"

"His name was Jose Maria Bonifacio Perez Cajeme, which means "he who does not drink." That is, he could go for long periods without water, making him difficult to catch; of course they eventually did find him and shot him by firing squad. I don't know when the great grandparents died, but I have a feeling they didn't live that long after being deported to Oaxaca. In 1925 grandfather married a young Yaqui woman also named Maria and my father, Jose Ignacio Perez, was born in 1927. When nineteen years old Father married a sixteen year old Yaqui/Zapotec girl in 1946 and they had five children in five years. I was number five born in 1951, the fourth girl, so no big deal. Then they also had another girl and two boys. In 1961 we moved to Mexico City for father to find work. In 1963 mother died when she was thirty-three, having had nine children in seventeen years.

I had to help raise the younger kids along with part time maids, some nice, but most of them nasty. We lived in a terribly poor neighborhood. At twelve I was a tall, thin, relatively fair skinned child. Most of the kids in the area were short and dark (many Zapotecs). They teased me incessantly, but I fought back. I really held my own against not only the girls but also the boys; I think it was my fierce heritage from Cajeme."

"Selena, you really have a good memory and lots of information about your family."

"That's from my father. He had a terrific memory and told me more than once all about our family. I'm really grateful he did. Now Terry, is that enough?"

"No, I still would like to hear about how you and Manuel got together. From what you told me your early life and Manuel's upbringing were worlds apart."

"OK Terry, let's have one more scotch and I will tell you the rest of my life story."

"Fine, I won't harass you for anymore details."

"So I'm twelve and my street brawls get more frequent and sometimes downright violent. I had learned some German from my father and in the heat of battle with the local rowdies I would call them names in German. Dumkof was fairly mild and they figured out what it meant. So I began to use my favorite insult, "du bist hundeschesse.""

"Selena I think I recognize that, something about dog shit?"

"Exactly, literally you are dog shit. My adversaries never figured it out, but some adults did and the next thing I knew I was in Catholic school. I don't know if the abuse from the street kids was any worse than the fire and brimstone rantings of some of the nuns."

"Fire and brimstone, does that mean going to hell?"

"Absolutely."

"Anyway, after five years I graduated (students called it escaping from purgatory) in 1968. Without bragging, I must tell you in those years I had blossomed into a darker, well built gal, and had begun to understand the value of my looks as a key to my future. After graduation I had a variety of odd jobs and eventually went to beauty school."

"What's beauty school?"

"Hair dressing, cutting and grooming women's hair.

One evening (I'm twenty) in a bar and every guy in the place is trying to get me into bed. I got really mad and cussed them all. A friend of mine who was with me, said "Selena you should get a job with the airlines as a stewardess; they want good looking women and I think you're a sure bet."

"So in 1971 I applied for a position and was hired immediately. Then in 1974 I met a guy named Manuel Silva on a flight from Mexico City to New York. It was very apparent at our first encounter that he was completely overwhelmed with, I assume my looks. He was so smitten he began arranging his trips on Aero Mexico when I was flying. I guessed that he was a guy with money by the way he dressed, some jewelry he wore and his tendency to buy other passengers drinks. I decided to do some research on him and discovered that his family likely had more money than God. The rest is history; we were married in 1975. Many folks and some media labled it the most lavish wedding of the year, maybe for the decade, in Mexico City. Then president Luis Echeverria Alvarez was in attendance at our wedding."

"Wow, quite a journey from a poverty -stricken waif from the barrio to the elegance of a palatial presidential mansion."

"Yes I suppose you could say that!"

Terry thought to himself, 'ah, as that wise guy Will Panzer would say, now we know who has the huevos in the family. Maybe old Manuel is even weaker and more malleable then I suspected. That's good to know.'

A SOULLESS MAN

June: 1998

President Manuel Silva was called to attend a national conference in Washington, DC. The meeting was to include the president's of institutions of higher education as well as other top officials of the schools. He left Corvallis Thursday morning June 4th for Washington.

The next day Selena spoke with Manuel and told him that she had decided to go to Eugene on Saturday, maybe to do some shopping at a new boutique that had just opened.

"Then I want to take the scenic highway 126 to Florence to walk in the white sand dunes. I could use a little time to myself and have a luscious seafood dinner at one of their many great restaurants. "

Manuel had reminded her to drive carefully on that road as there were stretches that could be quite dangerous.

"Oh don't worry dear I will be very careful."

Later that day she called Terry, who now lived in Eugene, and asked him if he would like to go with her to Florence on Saturday and return Sunday. Always cautious, he declined, telling her that in fact he was going up to Corvallis to do some work in his office over the weekend. However, Selena decided to surprise him the next day and see if he would change his mind. She arrived in Eugene late morning and purposefully parked a block away from his home. She quietly unlocked the front door with a key he had given her. When she silently entered his bedroom he was on his knees bent over prone and speaking Arabic as if in prayer-which he was. While Terry was surprised at her sudden appearance, by contrast, Selena was flabbergasted.

"Terry, Terry, what in the world are you doing?"

He bolted upright, whirled to face her, his face contorted in a mixture of total shock but also masked in rage.

"Selena what are you doing here and how did you get in the house?"

"With the key you gave me."

She paused momentarily and then blurted out, "Terry I think you were praying as a Muslim, and in fact I know you were. The mat you're praying on is called a Sajjada, a Muslim prayer rug. What does this mean? I don't believe what I'm seeing and she burst into tears. Terry, Terry!"

Ishmael composed himself, walked up to Selena, grasped her by the shoulders pulled her into a tight embrace and exclaimed "Selena, Selena stop crying I can explain this to you."

"Terry what is there to explain-are you a Muslim? Are you really who you say you are; should I be afraid of you?"

"Selena stop, you're getting hysterical for no reason. Here, sit down."

Ishmael was stunned, his heart thundering and his mind racing; he knew he had to gather his wits and quickly fabricate a story she would believe and calm her fears.

Selena was a highly intelligent woman, herself a master of deceit, and not easily duped.

He immediately understood that his future as Terry and the years planning for revenge against the abominable Jews was at this moment hanging in the balance.

"Oh Terry, she sobbed, what is going on?"

Having regained his composure, he steeled himself and began.

"Selena my love don't say or ask me anything more, I will explain the prayer rug and everything you want to know. I understand you must be shocked by what you've seen. I know it's not past noon here in Oregon but it is somewhere in the world, so why don't we both have a small libation to settle our nerves? Then I promise to be totally and completely honest with you. What about that drink?"

Selena visibly shivered, took a deep breath and said, "OK but make mine a double or even a triple."

Ishmael hurriedly fixed the drinks, scotch and water, and made Selena's about 80-20 scotch to water. He returned and sat down next to her on the sofa. Selena downed almost half of her drink in less than a minute while Ishmael sipped a small amount.

"Selena are you OK?"

"Well I don't know, I'm so confused."

"I know, I understand, but hear me out my love."

Ishmael paused for a few seconds and then began.

"Selena I'm really glad you came unannounced and surprised me this morning. I have been extremely stressed these past several months. I have spent many hours wrestling with being able to tell you about my life and who I am; have you noticed?"

"Yes I know that you have seemed very preoccupied recently, even when we made love. I was worried about you and wondering if you had become tired of me."

"Selena, you're a bright lady and I wondered if you recognized that I was deeply troubled."

"Well I did recognize that something was amiss."

"Now Selena listen carefully and I will explain everything; what I'm about to tell you no one else in this world knows.

Today I am a man called Terry Fitzroy, but I was born the son of a violent Egyptian Muslim and a wealthy American free spirit from California."

Selena gasped and interrupted, "but Terry you told me the story of your life at El Cisne, was all that not....?"

Terry stopped her in midsentence, "Selena wait, I know what I told you but now allow me to explain to you why. At birth I was given the name Mohammad Hassan. When I was twenty-one years old I changed my name to Terry Fitzroy."

"From Mohammad to Terry?"

"Yes I know it seems bizarre, but a man named Terry Fitzroy was the best friend I ever had; he saved my life."

"Terry, I don't understand; the scotch has really wasted me, but what you're telling me is incredible."

"I know but please listen to me. My father was a tyrant. He hated almost anyone who wasn't a Muslim; Jews, Christians, Buddhists, Hindus-everyone it seemed. He was harsh, demanding and abusive. I loved my mother and he knew it. I still carry guilt feelings that he was so cruel to her because of my devotion to her. He literally imprisoned her; he abused her, physically beat her and finally drove her into an institution, psychologicaly destroyed. She committed suicide when I was eleven years old and he blamed me for her death."

"Oh Terry this is awful."

"Yes it was; my mother had been good to me, but both of us were deathly afraid of him. He constantly drilled me on the Quran, making me memorize verse after verse. By the time I was fifteen years old I hated Islam and I suppose also my father. At that young age I began to drink alcohol, smoke cigarettes, blasphemy Allah-anything to violate the tenants of

Islam. And then in 1967 he was killed in the war with Israel. When I heard of his death it was a joyous day. I was sent to live with his brother and wife. She was as evil as my father and watched every move I made, even having her four children spy and report on me. When I was eighteen I ran away and ended up in Southeast Asia, working for an import/export company. I worked very hard in the company and with my initiatives and some maneuvering of which I'm not proud, I was able to buy the company. It was there that I met Terry Fitzroy, a brilliant and wonderful man. He recognized my struggles with my identity and listened to my deepest darkest feelings. He had become a strong Christian after the troubles in his life. He was a homosexual and estranged from his family. He became a trusted friend, a mentor, like a brother to me; then again tragedy struck my life. One evening Terry was found in an alley beaten to death. No charges were ever brought but the rumor was that he had died at the hands of young militant, violent anti-Christian Muslim hoodlums. I was devastated at the loss of my only friend and I contemplated suicide for several months."

Selena was weeping, "Oh Terry, that's terrible, how have you survived all of these tragedies?"

"I really don't know, but after Terry was killed I struggled even more with my identity; I had nightmares about being born a Muslim and now wanting to completely reject all of that ideology. Later the job opportunity at Oregon State became available and I was hired. Then we met and later I realized I had fallen in love with you. I didn't know what to do. I wanted to tell you about my past as I knew that I couldn't continue our relationship living a lie. I began to fantasize about a time when you would eventually leave Manuel and we could marry and live together. Sometimes I get so desperate I don't know what to do and that is what was happening when you just came in. I wondered what would happen if I tried some Islamic prayers. I also have attended some Christian services, the Catholic Church in Eugene and also a couple of Protestant congregations here in town. None of it seemed to help. Then I bought this Islamic prayer rug to see if it might bring answers-it didn't work. You see Selena I'm not a good Muslim, not really a Muslim at all. I'm not a follower of Islam in any sense. I drink alccohol, eat pork, have tattoos and don't observe or follow any of the Islamic tenets.

Selena sobbed and began to cry again.

"Selena, you don't have to say anything now. I can imagine my life and who I am must be mind-boggling, but Selena make sure you understand who I am; Terry Fitzroy, not the former abused child of a maniacal Muslim who destroyed my mother. He was also well on his way to obliterating my identity as a teenager struggling to grow into adulthood. I was the constant target of his criticism and punishment and then thankfully he was killed."

"Oh Terry your life must have been a living hell."

"Yes it was, what I recall was humiliation and pain. After grieving for months over the loss of my friend I made a decision to change my name to Terry Fitzroy to honor him and live the rest of my life as he might have; to forget, as best I could, the torturous reality of my early years. Selena in my heart and soul today I am Terry Fitzroy. Do you think I am insane?"

"Oh Terry no. I don't know how you survived all of that brutality and heartbreak. You're not crazy my love, just a man who has endured unspeakable tauma."

"Selena I have loved two women in my life, my mother and now you.

"Terry, Terry, this is all such a sudden shock. Right now I don't know what to say. I need time to think about our future together."

Ishmael relaxed, breathed a sigh of relief and thought, 'she believes me. As intelligent as she is she's also just like most females-they think with their emotions not their heads; praise to you Allah.'

Selena continued to cry, a whimper, sobbing softly.

"Selena are you OK?"

"Yes," she replied weakly. Ishmael mixed two more drinks, hers again 80-20 scotch to water. They sipped the drinks quietly and Selena lay down on the couch and fell asleep.

Ishmael sat next to her his mind racing as he thought of what he now must do. He was a student of history and Julius Caesar was one of his ancient heroes. As he contemplated his next moves, the Latin phrase that Caesar uttered when he crossed the Rubicon River with his army came to mind. He softly whispered aloud "Alea iacta est" (the die is cast); now there was no turning back for he and Selena.

Ishmael watched Selena for a brief time as she breathed heavily, likely in a state of semi -consciousness He thought, 'now I must act quickly and decisively. I must leave nothing to chance. What first?'

Initially he thought of a blanket-a thick one He retrieved a wool quilt from a closet and placed it under her. Now the car-I must get it into the garage. She had parked half a block from his house to surprise him and he realized what he must do; get the car out of sight when he loaded the contents for the final journey. He quickly found the car keys and silently slipped out of the house, got into the car, drove it into his garage and closed the garage door. He had encountered no one on the street and was sure he had not been observed.

Selena was still sleeping soundly when he entered the living room. He sat down next to her and gazed at her. What a woman you are he thought; 'a beautiful face, a wonderful lustful body, a creature of great pleasure.' He suddenly experienced a tremble, a dryness in his mouth and a twinge in his stomach. "No, no" he gasped aloud, "I must honor the almighty Allah and the code of Islam." He leaned over, gently lifted her up from the couch moving her back to his front side. He reached his arms around her neck as her head limply rolled to one side. She uttered a quiet moan as Ishmael violently twisted his arms and snapped her neck with an audible crack. She died instantly. He paused for a moment then gently pulled the blanket with Selena on it to the floor. Ishmael poured himself another scotch and water, sat down, and began a mental inventory of what needed to go into her car along with Selena. Her purse, the coat she was wearing, and the half bottle of Glenlevit scotch. From his garage he took four roadside emergency flares and placed two in the front seat and two in the trunk of her car.

He changed into his jogging clothes, dark colored shoes and a pack to carry water, a flashlight, a flask of scotch and a small .32 caliber pistol.

He waited silently for several hours and as it began to darken at sunset he placed Selena, her purse, her coat, her cell phone, and the bottle of scotch in the car. He drove to the edge of town and filled the car with gasoline using her credit card. No one was at the station. He silently thanked Allah knowing the almighty one was guiding his furtive departure from the city.

He knew the road, highway 126 to Florence, as he had driven it on several occasions. He drove for eleven or twelve miles until he came to a place with a series of sharp twisting turns. While roadside barriers covered most of the dangerous overlooks there were a number of locations where a vehicle could go over with careless driving. Ishmael stopped, listened for any oncoming traffic, hearing none he pulled the car perilously close to an unguarded overlook. He shifted the car into park, pushed her body to the drivers seat, hurriedly opening the trunk to ignite the flares. He quickly returned to the front of the car, ignited the flares in the front seat, placed the car in drive, and leaped out of the passenger door as it began to move. He watched it slip over the edge and begin to careen down the mountainside .

He raced across the road into the brushy hillside and waited, his heart pounding wildly. What seemed to him an agonizing lapse of time was finally rewarded as he heard a loud explosion and then a second blast. Still no traffic had approahed, and again he praised Allah. Then he saw a rising column of black smoke from the canyon below and was overcome with the urge to cross the road to view the scene. Against his better judgment he bolted from the sanctity of the brush, ran to the overlook and saw the vehicle fully engulfed in the gasoline fed fire. He again retreated back to the brush, and not a second too soon as two vehicles following closely appeared on the way to Florence. Miraculously they didn't slow as they apparently didn't observe the smoke that was clearly visible.

Ishmael remained silent, hidden in the brush for twenty to thirty minutes. Several more cars passed while he waited; much of the smoke had dissipated and none of them slowed or stopped. Feeling somewhat numb he further dampened his senses swallowing half the flask of scotch. He stepped onto the highway and began jogging back to Eugene. Each time he heard a vehicle approaching he jumped into the brush lining the road or flattened himself in a ditch or recession. Between dodging cars and stopping to rest occasionally, he didn't arrive back in Eugene until around 9:00 PM. He carefully picked his way through darkened side streets and encountered very few cars or cyclists before arriving at his home. He took a very hot shower, ate a small snack, crept into bed and soon fell asleep. He slept fitfully, waking repeatedly with a reoccurring hideous nightmare. He would bolt upright perspiring profusely with the image of a beautiful raven- haired soul pleading for redemption and shrieking for release from the flames of Hades.

"DEATH" Of A PRESIDENT

June: 1998

President Silva began to worry as he had not received any comunication from Selena since they spoke on Friday June fifth. It was Sunday morning and despite Manuel's repeated attempts to contact Selena her cell phone continued to go to voicemail. He then began to call their home in Corvallis and the answering machine clicked on with each attempt. Early Monday morning he contacted his executive assistant, Lynda Stapleton, asking her to go to his home to check on Selena. Within the hour Lynda called back to inform Manuel that she was not at home and furthermore that her black Mercedes was also not there. Manuel exclaimed, "oh no I know something bad has happened."

"Wait Manuel, don't think anything is wrong at this time; let me follow up on where Selena might be, including checking with her favorite seafood restaurant In Florence."

By Monday evening with no information on her whereabouts, Manuel called the Corvallis police department and also the Oregon State Police to report Selena as a missing person.

Growing increasingly frantic by the hour, he booked reservations the next day to fly back to Corvallis on Tuesday morning. Lynda met him at the airport, and immediately observed that he was in a state of near panic.

Manuel, unlike his assertive wife, was a gentle, mild mannered and trusting individual. He had been born into an extremely affluent family and throughout his life he enjoyed a privileged, carefree upbringing, rarely, if ever, being denied his needs or his wishes. Thus In June of 1998 with his financial future secure and his marriage to Selena in 1975, the combination of the two appeared to be an underlying source and strength of his emotional security. Manuel, however seemed to have little understanding of the powerful influence that Selena wielded in almost all of his personal and professional decision-making.

In the car on the way home, Manuel again began to question Lynda if she had learned any news concerning Selena.

"No I'm afraid not," she replied, recognizing that he was close to breaking down in tears.

"I know that something terrible has happened, she just can't have completely vanished."

He began to sob softly and exclaimed in a pathetic tone, "oh dear I don't know what to do."

"Now, now President Silva," Lynda replied, placing her hand on his shoulder, "try not to think about negative things; there can be many reasons why we haven't heard from her."

"Oh I pray to God, I hope so."

Lynda drove him home to the presidential mansion. It was indeed a palatial home as Manuel had built the house with his money. The university had agreed to allow him the extravagant expenditure on the home as Manuel offered to give title to the university at the conclusion of his tenure as president. The original idea for the home had come from the fertile mind of

Selena who continually envisioned new ways to capitalize on what she viewed as the limitless coffers of her doting husband. Lynda helped Manuel unload his luggage and got him settled.

Finally she asked, "President Silva is there anything more I can do for you now?"

"Oh my let me think; I'm not sure."

"When did you last eat Mr. President?"

"Well I had a light lunch on the plane, now four or five hours ago."

"Would you like me to order something for you, say from your favorite Italian restaurant?"

"Yes, that would be good, would you want to join me?"

"I'm sorry sir I have to get home to check on my spouse."

"OK, I understand, I'll be fine. I'm going to call Miranda our in- home cook/housekeeper and ask her to return tomorrow as Selena had given her a couple of days off. Also, I'll have Raphael our gardener come over, he will be good company here at home. Tomorrow, probably late morning I will come to the office; maybe we can come up with some ideas or information concerning her whereabouts."

"Good I will see you sometime tomorrow, and try not to think bad thoughts."

"Yes, I know, and thanks Lynda for your support."

As she drove away she thought, 'poor Manuel isn't a bad guy, actually he's really a nice person, but what an insecure man, and why? She wondered if the money and the affluence was somehow responsible for his pathetic state. Watching him, the image of a once vibrant flower came to mind, now wilting, with over- watering having depleted the nutrients of the plant; Manuel, showered throughout his life with wealth which seems to have leached the very essence of his soul.'

Midmorning a week later, June thirteenth, the chief of police of Eugene Oregon, and another officer accompanied by

Lynda and Fr. Dennis O'Leary, priest of Saint Mary's Catholic church in Corvallis, arrived at the home of Manuel Silva.

Personnel from the Eugene Oregon police department had originally contacted the president's office and when Lynda got the news she immediately reached out to Fr. O'Leary and arranged for him to go with them to deliver the news to Manuel. Manuel, a faithful Catholic, regularly attended the 12:30 PM Spanish language mass and was particularly fond of Fr. O'Leary. When they arrived Miranda answered the chiming doorbell and ushered them into the study where Manuel was reading. When he looked up and saw the group he dropped his book, froze momentarily, and then wailed, "oh no, please, I don't want to know why you are here." Fr. O'Leary sat down next to Manuel on the sofa and placed his arm on his shoulder saying "Manuel my son."

"Oh Father O'leary is she gone?"

"Manuel her Mercedes was discovered in a deep ravine some distance from Eugene; it had apparently left the road crashed and burned. However, the process of positive identification of the victim found in the vehicle is not yet complete. When they determined that the vehicle was registered to Selena the police called your office. Lynda and the rest of us felt that you should be apprised of the situation."

"Oh dear Jesus she's gone isn't she? How did this happen? Why was she on that road? I know, she was going to Florence."

Manuel began to cry uncontrolled, breathing heavily, taking in huge breaths.

"Manuel please, offered Fr. O'Leary."

Manuel crying, now almost hysterically, hyperventilated and collapsed.

"Call an ambulance Lynda directed, let's get him to the hospital."

The medics arrived shortly and transported Manuel to the

hospital emergency entrance.

He was heavily sedated during his stay in the hospital. Three days later when he was released his physician prescribed a relatively high dosage of anti-depressant medication. Also, a twenty-four hour live-in registered nurse was provided as Manuel's doctor feared he might be suicidal. Within days of returning home he requested and was granted a four month leave of absence from his position as president. The leave was to begin July first.

When Manuel returned home in early November Lynda asked him if it would be OK for her to drop in ocasionally during the next two weeks to check on his progress and advise him of any important university matters.

"Oh yes, please do Lynda; why don't you stop by every day during the week. It will be good to have your company."

"Very fine sir, I'll do that; say about 10:30 or 11:00 AM?"

"Yes, that would be a good time."

During the ensuing two weeks she arrived daily, but spent the majority of the time listening to Manuel as he wrestled with the loss of Selena. Lynda had uncommon listening skills and an exceptional understanding of human behavior. His grief was understandable as he grieved deeply in losing his wife. However, at times, Lynda had the sense of a child lamenting the loss of a mother.

On each occasion Lynda sought to bring attention to a pressing institutional matter, Manuel invariably dismissed the attempt, usually remarking "oh Lynda let's discuss that later or have Ralph handle that issue." Ralph Wilson was Vice President for Academic Affairs who was to serve as interim president in Manuel's absence.

Lynda was deeply concerned about the president's total unwillingness to address or even hear of important institutional matters. She was keenly aware of his acute emotional instability and his struggles with losing Selena. However, most disturbing to her was a reoccurring sense that in the Silva family there had been more than one death. The physical demise of Selena in a fiery crash and the psychological destruction of Manuel Silva from unyielding grief.

THE CONFIDANT

Terry Fitzroy: 1998

President Silva returned from his leave of absence on November first. His staff and colleagues who had not seen him in the past four months were appalled and dismayed at the appearance of the man who slowly ambled into his office. Manuel had lost a considerable amount of weight and his characteristic brown- toned skin appeared to have an almost grayish pallor. Even more disturbing was his seeming hesitancy in speaking; when he did, his voice carried a weak hollow whispering tone. The once jovial robust man now appeared like a robotic machine charading as a human being. Lynda, his staunch imperturbable executive assistant, who had not seen him for four to six weeks was shaken at his appearance and demeanor.

After the shock of the initial encounter subsided, Lynda got Manuel settled in his office and brought him coffee and his favorite prune danish. They sat and chatted for a brief period and she opened a folder, and carefully editing the contents, began to provide mostly mundane and inconsequential information. Surprisingly, and unannounced, there was a soft knock on the office door; it opened slightly and Terry Fitzroy showed his face and cheerfully said, "well good morning Manuel and Lynda." At the greeting Manuel stood up, smiled broadly, and replied, "my goodness Terry I didn't expect to see you this morning; come on in and have some coffee."

"Oh no Manuel, I just stopped to welcome you back, I don't want to interfere."

"Nonsense, you're not interfering, I insist you join us. Lynda let's get Terry some coffee and a danish."

"Good, I'll be right back. If I need to start a new pot it will take a few minutes."

"Don't hurry Lynda, it will give Terry and me a few minutes to catch up on a few matters."

As unprepared as she was for Manuel's appearance, she was even more surprised at the dramatic elevation in Manuel's mood when Terry arrived. 'What was that all about she pondered?' In fact Lynda needed to brew another batch of coffee. As she waited for the coffee, she reflected back on the brief interaction between Terry and the president. "That Terry, sometimes I wonder about him, she mused. I know he's a charmer and readily able to gain favor for something he wants, but the interruption and his rather blase interchange with the president left me a bit unsettled." She shook her head almost violently and chastised herself, "for god's sakes Lynda get a grip." The moment passed and she took the coffee and another danish into the president's office.

However, in the ensuing days it became apparent that a major transformation had occurred in the relationship between Terry and the president. Terry began to appear at the president's office, not daily, but frequently during the week work days. For Lynda, the most notable aspect of his visits, (usually not on the president's calendar), was the consisteny that Manuel readily admitted him into his office. One morning as she became increasingly curious of his visits, she decided to ask Terry about the purpose of his seemingly excessive trips to the "tower" (president's office). Surprisingly, he responded with a noticeable edge in the tone of his voice. "Why Lynda is that a problem for you?"

Taken aback she said, "well no, but you have to admit it's not usual or customary for someone to make repeated unannounced visits to the president's office."

Again his reply carried an even stronger sharpness. "My my Lynda, it sounds as if you must not approve of me coming to see the president; why don't you express your views to Manuel and see how he feels about the matter."

"No Terry, it's not a problem for me, I was just commenting on the frequency of your visits and also the fact that the president appears eager to see you."

"Lynda, not now, but let's have lunch one day soon and I think I can enlighten you about the nature of the situation, especially my relationship with the president and his with me. OK?"

"Well OK, I don't want to make this a big deal, just idle curiosity I guess."

"Maybe that's true. Hey I have to run, I'll call to set a good time to have lunch."

"Right; Terry don't take offense at my questions."

"Don't worry your lovely head, none taken."

When Terry had gone, she realized she was shaking and although perspiring felt cold. She thought, 'I don't know, I've never seen that side of Terry before and I'm not sure I like it.'

As Terry left heading across campus for another cup of coffee, he thought about the interaction with Lynda; wondering especially about her appearing to question the necessity/ validity of his frequent trips to the presidents office. A bit frustrated, he thought, 'I knew it, that is one smart bitch. She could be a problem; I need to do some serious thinking before the luncheon with her. Maybe I need to cut down on my visits to Manuel's office. I'll just call him and make arrangements to meet him elsewhere.'

Lynda left the office that day feeling somewhat distraught over the encounter with Terry earlier that morning. Characteristic of her perseverance and resolve in confronting questions/problems facing her, she began to formulate a plan to better understand the dynamics of the new Terry/Manuel relationship. She thought of Miranda Estrada, Manuel's live- in housekeeper. Lynda's father had been a political diplomat to South America (Brazil) and she had spent her younger formative years immersed in the customs, culture and language of the people. She spoke and wrote the Spanish language fluently and was often called upon as an interpreter, particularly in complicated legal proceedings. Miranda adored Lynda, and any occasion she came to the presidential mansion, Miranda took the opportunity to visit with her as long as she could stay.

Lynda called Miranda and asked if she would meet with her. She also requested that the meeting not be disclosed to either President Silva or Terry Fitzroy. They met a week later on a Sunday, Miranda's day off, at a small Mexican restaurant frequented mostly by local Hispanics. Lynda decided to risk being completely honest with Miranda regarding her curiosity with the startling new relationship between Manuel and Terry. She had barely finished explaining to Miranda why she wanted to meet when the "floodgates" opened. Miranda began a torrent of words opening with, "Lynda since you are being completely honest with me I must first ask you a question; are you good friends with Terry?"

"No Miranda, as a matter of fact I am not; furthermore his behavior, especially since the president has returned, concerns me a great deal."

"Yes, yes, I know what you mean. That man is up to something Lynda and I don't like or trust him. Oh I'm sorry to say that, but..."

Lynda interrupted and replied, "no that's OK Miranda, our conversation and this meeting is between the two of us. I can promise you."

"Oh muchas gracias senora."

"Miranda what makes you think he is up to something?"

"Well, while the president was on leave trying to get better, he came to the house almost every day. He always took the president into his den and closed the door. Once when I was serving them coffee, I knocked but they didn't hear me and I opened the door to go in. That man, Terry, was saying something like, "oh don't worry Manuel, I can take care of that and no one will ever know." Then he saw me, stopped and glared at me. He said in not a nice voice, "Miranda don't ever walk in again witout knocking and interrupt us."

"I'm terribly sorry, I did knock." The president looked at me like he wasn't very happy and said "I'll tell you what Miranda, from now on just call me on the intercom when you need to come in. OK?"

"Yes sir that would be fine."

"After that day, that man Terry, sometimes stared at me with a mean look and would not speak to me. He often brought bottles of liquor especially when he came late in the afternoon or early evening. By the time he left the president had too much to drink. Later he began to bring a large briefcase with him. I know it had papers being signed by the president, as one night opening the door he said, 'now Terry I did sign all of the copies didn't I?' Again he gave me a very scary look, turned, and closed the door. I immediately went upstairs to avoid him."

Buy the end of their meeting and discussion it was apparent to Lynda that Terry Fitzroy not only had an agenda in mind, but even more concerning, she began to feel that he was a much more complicated individual than she had imagined. A soft silent whisp of fear enveloped her. She almost cried thinking, I almost believe he's dangerous. I need to be careful and stay away from him.

Notwithstanding her misgivings about Terry, she did agree to have lunch with him the week following her visit with Miranda. Terry met her with one of his characteristic sexually embroidered greetings.

"Wow, what a woman Lynda, you're looking amazing these days; it makes me want to steal you away to a deserted tropical island."

Lynda flinched for a second, recovered, and replied "yes, I know and I'd guess you try those lines on every woman you meet."

"No, not true Lynda. You have to know that you are close to the top of the scale in attractive women."

'Here we go,' she thought, 'he must have decided he needs something or is aware that he more than ruffled my feathers.'

"Okay, let's not quibble over the matter, I'm interested in learning what you have to say, as you memtioned, to clarify some issues."

"Good, hey let's order and I'll get on with my thoughts."

When lunch arrived Terry began.

"Lynda first of all with what I'm going to share you must agree to hold in strictest confidence. Manuel and I have discussed the subject and he wants the decision he's made kept quiet for now. Agreed?"

"Fine. As I understand, you say the president wishes total confidentiality at this point?"

"Yes absolutely."

"Very well."

"Lynda, the president has asked me to serve as a special

executive assistant to him in all major institutional policies and administrative decisions. During his leave of absence we spent considerable time discussing university matters and throughout those conversations, almost invariably, he would ask for my assessment, reactions and input on decisions he had made or intended to make. Apparently, well more accurately obviously, what he heard from me he felt demonstrated a high level of understanding and insight into the workings of a major educational institution, i.e., Oregon State University. He said he wanted to wait until the new fiscal year 1999 to make the position official. That would ensure not having the International Students Office accusing him of being, lets say a corporate raider. Ha! Along with not causing friction with that office there were additional issues; funding, and fleshing out the position that he felt dictated his decision be kept confidential at this point. My impending position and other matters of concern for him are the major reasons for the frequency of my trips to see him."

Lynda was stunned. She thought, 'I would have never guessed what Terry just told me; he is indeed a man of many surprises.' She composed herself and responded, "my goodness that is quite a bombshell; a good one I'd think. Congratulations, it would appear that you have gained the complete trust and confidence of the president."

"Thanks, you know we are now working on the agenda for the trip to Israel before the expected official opening in February 1999. Myself, Manuel, Panzer and O'Connell along with some individuals the president feels would be good additions for the trip will be announced later. Maybe you should accompany us. I will mention that to Manuel."

Lynda felt faint with her mind tumbling. Intuitively she sensed that Terry may have seized a major portion of control for the direction and future of the institution. Most frightening was the likelihood that the president was oblivious to the transfer of power.

PRESIDENT SILVA VISITS THE GAN

December: 1998

Will Panzer and Kevin O'Connell were both surprised with President Silva's opening statement.

"Gentlemen pack your bags we are leaving for Israel in less than three days."

The other two members present, Terry Fitzroy and Lynda Stapleton already knew of the trip and both smiled at Will and Kevin's reaction.

President Silva continued, "Terry and I feel we need to see the project now to discuss arrangements for the opening ceremonies and banquet this coming February.

Today is the eleventh and Lynda has already booked flights for us to arrive in Tel Aviv on Tuesday December fifteenth."

Kevin said, "my goodness I had no idea that the timing of the trip was being discussed."

"I know", replied the president, "but Terry and I were talking about getting everyone together and suddenly we had the whole schedule laid out and saw no reason for all of us to meet. Earlier I was able to speak with U.S. Senator Ron Wyden and also State Senator Earl Blumenauer and they were available to also make the trip."

"Yes I understand said Kevin."

Will decided to hold his tongue, but thought 'I think that Fitzroy is a sneaky prick. He didn't have a damn thing to do with the project, but somehow it would appear he's got the president completely snowed.'

"Lynda why don't you run through the itinerary for the trip. She'll also give each one of us a written copy of everything."

Lynda said, "listen carefully guys, its first class all the way so make sure you get this all down. President Silva has ordered two limousines for our eighty mile trip to Portland which leaves at 6:00 AM sharp from the president's home. We will board a Delta Boeing 757 at 10:00 AM to JFK, arriving 6:00 PM local time. The final leg is on EL AL, a 747-400 leaving at 10:00 PM and arriving at Ben Gurion Airport at 3:00 PM, again local time. Do be on time we will not wait. Any questions?"

No one had a question, but again Will thought, 'Jesus Christ lady this isn't my first ride in a limousine or flight on an airline; I do understand that both have designated departure times.'

The ride to Portland and then the flight to JFK was absent any problems and in fact turned out to be quite enjoyable for the group, as they were the recepients of special attention, complements of the senior pilot.

President Silva had pulled off a minor coup. He had personally selected the date and time of the flight to JFK as the pilot was his nephew, Captain Ricardo Lorenzo Silva. Ricardo was an ex-navy jet pilot from Mexico and a graduate of the U.S. Naval academy. Ricardo and the flight crew provided "celebrity-like" considerations for his uncle and his first class traveling companions, with frequent visits to chat along with free drinks. Unlike the plane, the light-hearted group landed in New York "fully-fueled."

They stayed overnight in Tel Aviv and the next morning left early for the one hour plus drive to the project site, some ninety miles from Tel Aviv. It was located at the northern area of the Negev, in the Arava Valley, twenty miles south of Beershba. The Israelis had selected the name of the project; they called it the Gan, which in Hebrew means garden. The word was first used in Genesis for the garden of Eden; It comes from the root ganan, that means to surround or defend. It would indicate that the Hebrew idea of a garden was an enclosed area perhaps like a walled garden.

Upon their arrival they noted that the Gan was indeed walled with a bristling eight to ten foot razor wire topped electric fence surrounding the facility; armed guards were also noted within the perimeter of the complex. Will, not shy in expressing his thoughts, gasped, "you have to be kidding, this place looks more like a penal institution for terrorists then a tilapia fish project."

President Silva visibly slumped in his seat and rather weakly replied, "Will please, we are guests of the nation of Israel and the exterior design of the facility we left to them."

Terry was more forceful. "Will I can see what you mean, but don't raise issues or make those kind of remarks as they can only lead to defensiveness and create ill will."

"That's right," echoed President Silva.

Will didn't comment further but again thought, 'what the hell's with Fitzroy these days, sounds like he's the head of this delegation and our spokesman; the president, I can't decide who's leading who around by their dick'.

Without further discussion they were ushered into a facility and met by Menachem Allon the project site diector and Noya Siegel, director of public relations. Will elbowed Kevin in the ribs and whispered quietly "watch this." As they had previously met Noya (which in Hebrew means divine beauty), Will anticipated the group's reaction, especially the men, when Noya appeared. Menachem uttered a guttural "good to see you", but Noya's greeting, "welcome to the Gan" sounded lyrical and her enchanting beauty caused a visible wilting of the assembled males. Will and Kevin both ambled in rather breezily and responded "hey Noya, how are you doing?" The rest of the guys fumbled, fawned and generally make fools of themselves over Noya. Both she and Menachem were keenly aware of the impact on individuals when they initially met this Miss Israel. Her beauty was indeed divine.

Will using the excuse that the devil was manipulating his thinking quietly whispered to Kevin.

"I'll bet these Israeli women are not like the rich Jewish women in America. You know gals that we call "Japs." I'd guess these ladies from Israel are real women and a riot in bed."

"Japs, what is that?"

"A Jewish American Princess. I'm surprised you never heard that before."

"OK, now I suppose you're going to tell me, how they are different?"

"Well of course; in America you can only tell that a Jewish American Princess has experienced an orgasm during sex when she drops her fingernail file."

"I don't believe it; Will, please stop with all these off-color jokes. They are great in a bar after a dozen beers, but not now."

Once in the facility, they met David Akkerman security director, Eli Effron, construction manager, Ben Adelman, aide to Netanyahu, and David Landau, who had been identified previously as a member of the project advisory committee.

They were served a luncheon featuring chilie encrusted tilapia and a wonderful selection of vegetables grown on site.

The afternoon and early evening was spent touring the facilities and preliminary discussions concerning the opening ceremonies and the banquet projected for February 1999. That evening they were treated to a musical interlude; a number of violin solos by David Landau and also several vocal solos by Noya who's singing talents were also breathtaking.

As the performances ended, Will took Terry aside and quietly said, "you know now is a good time to float the Ray Charles/David Landau duet idea."

"Hell no Will. I never really was for that idea and after I mentioned it to the president he agreed it was totally inappropriate."

"Well I still think it would be a knockout."

"No, absolutely not."

Will paused and thought to himself, ' bullshit, I'll bet Terry never approached the president. I just can't figure out what is going on between him and old Manuel.'

The following day, the seventeenth, discussions and planning for the upcoming ceremonies consumed most of the day. A principle participant in almost all of the issues was David Landau. Security was a primary focus for him, but he also demonstrated a keen perspective on seemingly every matter and function of the proposed day long celebration. He asked incisive questions concerning attendees (country and background) general questions regarding the day's agenda (hour by hour) the banquet, including menu, servers, and importantly seating arrangements, particularly at the head table. Some of the American group found Landau's repeated questions tiring and unproductive. Terry was silently seething. He fumed to himself thinking 'what the hell is with that damn Jew? He behaves like he thinks, or maybe he does, have a significant role in the project.'

Most of the individual differences in arrangements and the

agenda for the banquet were resolved without much discussion with the exception of one matter-seating arrangements at the head table. Terry had been the primary spokesman for Oregon State and readily conceded to the Israelis where differences surfaced. However, on the matter of who and where each individual would be seated he was adamant (Landau thought belligerent) that his ideas be followed. Eventually the group did agree with some minor grumblings.

As the discussion concerning seating unfolded David's radar-like brain receptors began to vibrate as he listened and carefully observed Terry's body language and demeanor. His feelings were not only uncomfortable, but at times sent chills throughout his body. As Terry held fast to his inflexibility concerning the seating situation, David thought, who is this fellow, and why he is he so insistent on where people are seated? Maybe I should have a discussion with the woman Lynda; she appears to be a bright intelligence lady and is close to the president and most likely this Terry. While listening to Terry's reasons why the seating placement was important, his mind wandered and then he recalled an incident earlier in the day when he happened to see Terry and Abasi Aziz, who managed the ornamental plants greenhouse, in conversation in that facility. He dismissed the incident at the time, but now again his intuitive instincts began to gnaw at him.

David did have the opportunity to speak with Lynda over drinks that evening. He was direct in asking about Terry, sharing his surprise at the apparent major role and impact that he had in the project.

"I understood he was a fulltime staff member in the International Students Office at Oregon State. Furthermore, it was my impression that he had no direct role in development of this project. Is that basically correct?"

David's initial questions left Lynda a bit uncomfortable

and somewhat intimidated. She rather weakly replied "yes you could say that." Throughout the day she had observed the probing, penetrating incisive nature of Landau's inquiries. It was apparent to her that not even the most insignificant details of the planning for the celebration would escape his scrutiny. She was unsure to what extent she should share her own misgivings of Terry, but David with his carefully worded, benign questioning, had gained enough information to heighten his level of concern for Terry's intentions.

Their conversation ended cordially with Lynda providing mostly factual information about Terry and his work activities at OSU. David, with his superbly honed observational skills, had garnered the essence of the information he sought. However, both he and Lynda departed veiled in a sinister cloud of foreboding.

Early Friday morning, the eighteenth, the Oregon group left the Gan for Jerusalem. They spent the day touring the old city on a hurried pace. A final stop was at the wailing wall. Will, always with an anecdote, stopped Kevin and asked, "did you hear about the American reporter who came to Israel to interview an older Jewish fellow; he had been praying at the wall some twenty to thirty years for world peace?"

Kevin winced and replied, "Will, what is your need to trivialize every event with I'd guess more off-color humor? OK, tell me and get it over with."

"This female correspondent asked the old man, do you believe your prayers have had any impact on reducing worldwide conflicts?"

The old man sighed and replied, "no not really."

"Why do you say that sir?"

"Well frankly it's because after all these years all I can conclude is that I've been talking to a wall."

Kevin didn't laugh, just rolled his eyes, weakly replying,

"ok I get it."

Saturday morning they left Tel Aviv for the twelve hour flight to JFK. At 8:30 PM-EST they headed for Portland arriving at 11:15 PM-PST. President Silva had the limousines waiting for the trip back to his residence in Corvallis. They all spent the night at his presidential home and were treated to a catered breakfast the next morning. Everyone thanked the president profusely for his hospitality and all agreed that the trip was a major success.

One Terry Fitzroy by name, but in reality and spiritually a man possessed, Ishmael Abboud, was elated, almost euphoric. He now envisioned that his thirty year quest for revenge for the murder of his parents was imminent. Soon Israel would suffer retribution for the heinous act that still haunted his dreams.

JOY AND DESPAIR

The Gan-February: 1999

Guests began to arrive on Friday February fifth, 1999 for the two day celebration and dedication

of the joint Oregon State Univerity/Israeli Tilapia project, the Gan. The attendees truly had an international flavor as individuals from Europe, Asia, Africa, the Middle East, South America, Cuba, and of course Israel and the United States were in attendance. Although temporary sleeping quarters were provided, (modular and "tent cities"), some guests elected to stay overnight in Beersheba and commute daily.

Media outlets, newspapers and television had also sent personnel for the dedication. Major newspaper coverage was provided by Haaretz (Israel), and the Corvallis-Gazette times. Television coverage included Israeli National television, the BBC, and NBC (USA) who sent a newly employed special events reporter.

The weather cooperated, sunny in the sixties during the day and lows in the mid forties during the night. The atmosphere was festive with the main banquet hall adorned with flowers, many pictures of the initial groundbreaking ceremonies and also full color photos of progress to completion. Large flags of nations involved in the development of the project fluttered on the exterior of the hall. During the day, snacks and a variety of drinks were provided, featuring fruits and vegetables (grown on site), along with breads and cheeses. It was apparent to arriving guests that no expense had been spared for the occasion.

Friday evening a light buffet dinner was provided and a short program included a welcome by Menachem Allon, introduction of notable guests, and the itinerary for the following day. the highlights for Saturday would be the dedication of the Gan and the banquet as concluding events. Once again the Israelis had orchestrated a coup for the event as prime minister Benjamin Netanyahu would give a blessing and the dedication address.

The American contingent to the event included: President Silva, Will Panzer and spouse, Kevin O'Connell and his wife, Lynda Stapleton and husband, Terry Fitzroy, U.S. Senator Ron Wyden, Oregon State Senator Earl Blumenauer, a young woman and man of Jewish faith from Israel who were attending Oregon State University and a reporter from the Corvallis Gazette -Times. Counting heads prompted Will to remark, "holy smokes thirteen, I hope that's not a bad omen; maybe Lynda should have brought her Schnauzer Willie so we could count him as number fourteen."

Lynda was prepared for Will's flippancy and remarked, "oh Will I didn't realize you were suffering from triskaidephobia?"

"What's that?"

"Never mind, you can look it up when we get back to Oregon." They all laughed and continued to mingle, devour snacks, and make certain their glasses were replenished with their favorite drinks.

Almost everyone appeared to fully enjoy the day. There

were, however, two exceptions to the total merriment. David Landau was cautious and continually surveying his surroundings for even the slightest indication that mischief could be afoot. He had spoken to Menachem late in the afternoon of his concerns about the large number of people in a relatively small location; specifically the inability to account for the behavior of any one individual. Menachem almost scoffed at David's trepidations.

"Look David, we have plenty of security and in general we literally know every attendee and their backgrounds. While I also take security seriously, at this time my only comment is, in the name of Yahweh relax." That ended their discussion of security for the duration of the event.

Terry was also very much unsettled. He had rehearsed his plan for the event repeatedly. Each time he went through the planed sequence of events for each day he carefully evaluated what alternatives might be available if a last minute change was required. After exhausting all the possible contingencies he could think of, psychologically exhausted himself, he numbed his tensions over tomorrow's events and refreshed his spirits with an uncounted number of Cragganmore single malt scotch whiskies.

The evening's entertainment, totally orchestrated by the Israelis was a resounding success. Miss Israel, Noya Siegel, began with a number of vocal solos; some in English, others mostly in Hebrew, that left the audience spellbound with her electrifying lyric soprano voice. Following Noya was a troupe of Israeli folk dancers from Tel Aviv University. Among the lively and spirited dances was the popular Hora (circle dance). Their performance conveyed a mood of freedom and celebration and the joy of youth. David Landau was the final act for the evening, thrilling his audience with two classic violin solos; Bach's Parita No.1 in B minor and Paganini's Caprice No. 5.

He ended the performance with his exhilarating rendition of Hava Nagila. It was indeed a joyous evening for almost everyone with the exception of one troubled dark soul who spent a restless night of anticipation.

Saturday morning began with activity bustling throughout the complex. The early agenda included various workshops on growing systems for tilapia, shrimp, vegetables, ornamental flowers, fruits and exotic plants. Other presentations were lectures on the construction and operation of the facilities including materials for fabrication, machinery, power systems, research trials, data collection, and analysis of costs. Additionally, there were guided tours of the facilities provided by key Gan staff with a focus on question and answer sessions for the participants. The morning activities seemed to move at a rapid pace and suddenly it was midday and again a light lunch was provided which ended at around 2:00 PM.

As the culmination of the two day celebration was to begin at 6:00 PM that evening, the invited guests were released from the scheduled activities. However, there was a growing palpable sense of anticipation for the 4:00 PM arrival of prime minister Benjamin Netanyahu. While all of the assembled knew of his impending appearance they were told he would not mingle with them, instead go into seclusion with key Gan staff to discuss plans for his dedication address at approximately 6:15 PM. Excitement for many was simply the opportunity to see Netanyahu. However, for others, his impending arrival elicited far stronger emotions. Terry Fitzroy experienced a deepening sense of exhilaration as he foresaw his thirty year quest for vengeance was imminent. David landau's feelings of foreboding seemed to heighten with each passing minute. All of his visceral instincts were pulsating through his body; he simply could not dispel a feeling of impending disaster. Will Panzer, the master of the improbable, relaxing with Kevin and Lynda holding a single malt whisky in hand, remarked, "Hey what's the chance we might get to meet old Bibi, maybe even shake his hand."

Kevin barked, "not a chance in hell Panzer-don't even ask things like that."

"OK OK, relax Kevin, just a little levity for the evening."

Almost on the hour, 4:00 PM, the unmistakable hum of helicopters in the distance was detected. It was Netanyahu arriving in a Sikorsky Blackhawk U-l60 A; likely one of ten surplus Blackhawks sold to Israel in 1994 that Netanyahu apparently requisitioned for his use. However two additional helicopters also arrived, AH- 1 W super Cobra gunships escorting the Blackhawk for security. All three landed but only the occupants of the Blackhawk, Netanyahu and six security personnel deplaned and were rapidly escorted away to a room adjacent to the banquet hall. The crowd cheered mightily at the appearance of the prime minister, but he only smiled broadly, waved, and hustled into the meeting room. Menachem Allon and David Landau also both entered the room. Seeing Landau disappear into the interior, Terry winced and thought to himself, 'that bastard Landau is more than just a member of a project advisory committee. Who the devil is he and what is the up to?'

Inside the very private meeting room Menachem briefly outlined the agenda for the dedication and the banquet. Prior to Netanyahu arriving David had spoken with Allon expressing concern over the seating placements of guests at the head table. He insisted that the topic and the placement of each individual be reviewed. Allon was initially reluctant to have the matter discussed, but Landau was adamant and Menachem relented. He then called on Landau to share his concerns about the seating arrangements.

Landau spoke.

"First of all Terry Fitzroy of the American group established the seating placements. He alone made the decisions and frankly I don't trust him. I attempted to research his background and found little information. Also a key staff member of Oregon State University where he works also shared that she had major concerns about his often evasi behavior in discussing his past. Simply said, I have an unabated feeling that he is dangerous. I will admit it is again my intuition, but based on my past experiences, I cannot ignore what I interpret as warning signals. My specific concern is that Fitzroy has grouped most of the Israelis together. Why? I don't understand, and I believe it is significant. Let me show you a layout of Fitzroy's idea for the seating."

Fitzroy's arrangement had Allon, master of ceremonies centered at the table. To his left, in order, were Netanyahu, David Akkerman-security director, Efrem Glick-production manager, the representative from the Jewish national fund, Kevin O'Connell-USA, Eli Effron- construction manager, President Manuel Silva-US and the representative from the Gates-Buffet foundation. On Allon's right were Will Panzer-USA, Aaron Eisen-hatchery manager, Ben Adelman-aide to Netanyahu, the U.S. Department of Agriculture representative, U.S. Senator Ron Wyden, and finally the two members of the international advisory committee Dr. Graciela Soto of Cuba and the world renowned expert in shrimp pathology, Dr. Don Lightner of the University of Arizona's Environmental Research Laboratory.

"As you can see seven Israelis essentially occupy the center of the table; In contrast, only three of the American representatives are centrally located."

Rather harshly Allon replied, "so what?"

"Again I admit I don't know," replied Landau.

"David this is not the time to argue over this matter. You

give us your arrangement and we'll go with it. Everyone OK with that? Oh, by the way, don't move me, as master of ceremonies I'm staying in the center spot."

There was no disagreement and Landau gave each his layout for the seating arrangement. It was as follows: Allon again centered. To his left Kevin O'Connell -USA, the representative of the Jewish national fund, the representative from the Gates-Buffet fund, Ben Adelman-aide to Netanyahu, Effrem Glick-production manager, David Akkerman-director of security, President Manuel Silva-USA, and prime minister Benjamin Netanyahu.

Seated on the right side of Allon were Will Panzer-USA, the U.S. Dept of agriculture representative, Eli Effron-construction manager, Aaron Eisen-hatchery manager, U.S. Senator Ron Wyden, Dr. Graciela Soto-Cuba, and Dr. Don Lightner-USA.

Landau added, "if anyone has questions concerning the changes we tell them it better reflects the primary principals who brought the project to fruition."

At 6:00 PM sharp Menachem called everyone to attention with a hearty welcome.

"What a wonderful joyous day, I'm so pleased to see all of you here today. Isn't everything lovely-especially the flowers on the table. They are varieties of Bromeliads, a favorite of Abasi Aziz who grows them here in our facilities. The fresh pineapple we served you for lunch was from one of our Bromeliads. No more speeches from me right now only to introduce a beautiful young woman, Noya Siegel, Miss Israel, who will honor both America and the nation of Israel by singing their national anthems. First the American anthem and then the Hativah (The Hope)."

Noya stepped to the podium and her only word was "shalom." With the completion of the anthems many in the audience had been brought to tears with her spectacular renditions.

When Allon returned to the podium it was apparent he also had been emotionally moved by her singing.

"ladies and gentlemen there is nothing I can add after that performance," and the audience again burst into applause. Allon continued, "now it is my distinct honor to introduce prime minister Benjamin Netanyahu, who will deliver a blessing and a brief dedication for the official opening of the Gan."

Netanyahu came out of the meeting room, walked quickly to the podium, also uttered a firm shalom and began his remarks which lasted between five and seven minutes. He thanked everyone for their attendance and stepped away from the podium. Allon announced, "OK all of the honored guests who will be seated at the head table please come forward now and find your location."

Terry lurking at the back of the hall, tensed and thought to himself, 'now the hour has arrived, praised be to Allah.' As Netanyahu approached the table he was intercepted by a Gan staff member. Several other staff joined the now milling group being directed to the revised seating arrangement. Suddenly Terry realized what was occurring-a complete overhaul of his seating plan had taken place. Shocked, he thought, 'what is happening? Who is responsible for these changes?'

In the midst of the confusion Allon explained "sorry everyone we had a last minute change in assigned seats, but we will be ready to go in a second or so." With everyone settled and Netanyahu seated the furthest from the center of the table, Terry realized that his plans had somehow been compromised. With every fiber in his body shrieking in outrage, feeling he had lost his very soul, he murmured softly to himself "it must be now" and he pressed a button on his cell phone. Almost at the same moment David Landau experienced a sickening awareness; he cried aloud "oh no it's the flowers, the potted plants, how could I have not seen that?"

A thunderous explosion obliterated the center section of the head table. The hall was filled with smoke, wood and metal fragments and glass shards flying in all directions. However, most horrifying was the multiple body parts showering the table and individuals sitting in the first several rows of the audience. Menachem Allon, Will Panzer, Kevin O'Connell, the representative of the Jewish National fund, Eli Effron, the U.S. Dept of agriculture representative and Aaron Eisen were killed instantly by the blast. Several ounces of Semtex (in America C-4) hidden in the base of the two Bromeliad potted plants sitting on the table on either side of Allon carried the wrath of destruction. There were many who suffered life-threatening trauma, and others with minor injuries. The lights went out in the hall and a series of additional explosions were heard throughout the complex. Chaos and hysteria reigned; individuals shouting, screaming and running amok with no apparent direction. However, at the moment of the initial blast Netanyahu's six security personnel emerged from the side meeting room, helped up a badly shaken but uninjured prime minister, and raced toward the helicopter already beginning to power up. They all boarded and were airborne in less than ten minutes. The Cobras left almost simultaneously.

After transmitting the deadly signal of murder and mayhem, Terry quickly exited the hall and ran toward a gated side entrance of the complex. He joined Abasi Aziz who was waiting in an unmarked Gan delivery truck with the engine running. They pulled up to the gate where the guard recognized Aziz and asked, "Abasi what is happening?"

Aziz replied, "I don't know, but it's not good." He pulled a handgun from under his coat and shot the guard in the forehead. Terry pulled the body aside and Abasi unlocked the gate and swung it open. They jumped into the van, left the facility and disappeared into the darkness; apparently unnoticed with much of the complex in complete chaos and a number of buildings now in flames. A delivery truck leaving the grounds was not observed or simply ignored.

A morning that had begun with joy and celebration, was now the scene of total shock and unspeakable grieving. The following day, news of the tragedy of the Gan spread like wildfire world-wide. Within a month President Silva and representatives of the Netanyahu administration agreed that rebuilding of the Gan would be permanently delayed at this time.

Weeks later, two men with widely disparate world-views sat alone with their thoughts. In Jerusalem, David Landau wept silently for the blood spilled by his countrymen and colleagues. He vowed to Yahweh he would find the man known as Terry Fitzroy. He thought 'we will strip his cloak of evil deceit and he will then atone for his sins in the halls of Israeli justice.'

Ishmael Abboud seethed silently in the city of Cairo, Egypt; trembling he thought, 'Netanyahu lives only because of that crippled Jew dog.' Then he swore an oath to the mighty one that he would again encounter Landau. "On that day he will know the full fury of The Sword of Allah."

Acknowledgements

First of all I want to mention Dr. Kevin Fitzsimmons who I met with in 2013 about the idea for this book. Kevin is an internationally known professional with expertise in greenhouse aquaculture. His response was positive and he encouraged me to move ahead with the project. He also agreed to assist me through completion of the book. He did keep his promise, continuing to provide invaluable insight and assistance; including a period of several months when he was detained by the government of Myanmar, confined to a small compound and not allowed to leave. Obviously, his commitment was the key that jump started the process.

On matters of Jewish faith and the culture of Israel, two individuals provided suggestions and valuable insights in the initial drafts of the novel. Each of them was at one time director of the Weintraub Israel Center in Tucson, Arizona. Inbal Shitivi served in that capacity from 2019 to 2020. Abbii Cook has been the director from 2022 to the present time.

In past writings my wife Marlys and our good friend Sue

Poppaw served as primary proofreaders. Although they have both left us, I did find another accomplished proofreader. My sister Carol Silva agreed to read the entire manuscript. She corrected a good numer of spelling, puncuation and gramatical errors. As I recall she "volunteered" as I doubt there was any coercion or sympathy appeal on my part.

A great resource for me in past writings has been my son Matthew. Again with this book, I likely would not have finished it without his input. With his background in legal training/writing and command of the English language, he reshaped a number of chapters. He also recommended elimination of almost three chapters of the novel which he described as "not contributing to the development of the narratives." He was correct, as much of the information was tangential and distracted from the storyline. Additionally, on frequent occasions he rescued me from my computer technology snafus.

I struggled mightily trying to compose a succinct summary; as the professional writers say, "create a hook" that would capture a potential readers attention. Making little progress I called upon my neighbor and good friend Sharon Jensen. Her observations and recomedations were very incisive and I was able to reorganize the text and eliminate half of the original draft. Many thanks.

About the Author

Dr. Kent Kloepping earned a Doctorate in Rehabilitation and Counseling Psychology from the University of Arizona in 1972. He retired from the university and private practice in 1998. In 2006 he published a memoir, "The Upside Of The Downside," a chronicle of his life after contracting poliomyelitis at the age of seven in 1945. The focus of the book details the many support systems; family, friends, playmates, relatives and community organizations (The Upside) that were instrumental in his recovery from polio, (The Downside). Each of them contrbuted to his ablity to lead essentially a "normal," productive life.

His second publication in 2012, "Whimsical Wanderings" is a selection of his poetry and short stories. The anecdotal collection covers diverse topical themes including: Memories of Youth; Foreign Affairs; Dogs and Cats of Note, and Home in The Old Pueblo.

A third book, "A Century Long Journey To The Day Of Redemption" (with Gene Shippy) is a game by game description and analysis of the 2016 Chicago Cubs historic run to become baseball's World Series Champions after a 108 year hiatus.

The Sword of Allah is his first novel of fiction completed in the summer of 2023.